MURDER AT
SKULL HOUSEE

ELLERY PAGE IS BACK—
AND IN HOT WATER!

Unlike everyone else in Pirate's Cove,
Ellery Page, aspiring screenwriter,
reigning Scrabble champion,
and occasionally clueless owner
of the village's only mystery bookstore,
is anything but thrilled when
famed horror author Brandon Abbott
announces he's purchased legendary
Skull House and plans
to live there permanently.

Ellery and Brandon have history.
Their relationship ended badly,
and the last thing Ellery wants
is a chance to patch things up—
especially when his relationship
with Police Chief Jack Carson
is just getting interesting...

SECRET AT SKULL HOUSE

SECRETS & SCRABBLE BOOK TWO

JOSH LANYON

VELLICHOR BOOKS

An imprint of JustJoshin Publishing, Inc.

To my readers. Stay safe. Stay smart. Sail on.

SECRET AT SKULL HOUSE: AN M/M COZY MYSTERY
(Secrets and Scrabble Book 2)
May 2020
Copyright (c) 2020 by Josh Lanyon
Edited by Keren Reed
Cover and book design by Kevin Burton Smith
All rights reserved.

ISBN: 978-1-945802-64-5
Published in the United States of America

JustJoshin Publishing, Inc.
3053 Rancho Vista Blvd.
Suite 116
Palmdale, CA 93551
www.joshlanyon.com

A ship in harbor is safe, but that is not what ships are built for.

John A. Shedd

CHAPTER ONE

Murder is fun.

At least, a lot of otherwise nice, normal people seemed to think so. Having recently gone through the ghastly experience of finding a body in his bookshop—oh, and of being suspected of murder—Ellery Page was less thrilled by the notion of violent death. He couldn't deny it was good for business, though.

Something about the idea of murder in a mystery bookstore really captured people's imagination. True, a third of the tourists wandering into the Crow's Nest this beautiful sunny June morning were there specifically to see Where It Happened. But because they felt a little guilty for their ghoulishness, they almost always bought a couple of books before they left. So while business wasn't booming, it had certainly picked up.

Which was a good thing because Ellery's screenwriting career was going nowhere fast. He glanced down again at the latest rejection letter from his agent.

The worst part was, while the rejection stung—rejection always stings, even when you're getting rejected by people *you* would reject—he just couldn't get too worked up about it. Not on such a beautiful day.

And it *was* a beautiful day. Like a painting by one of those 19th century artists who went in for seaside postcards of gentlemen in straw hats and striped one-piece bathing suits and ladies with—well, frankly, Ellery was more interested in the gentlemen.

Anyway, really nice weather. The sky was a soft and languid blue, swirled with clouds as filmy as smoke. The sand sparkled, the water sparkled, the sunlight sparkled. Brightly colored boats bobbed in the harbor, flags snapping in the sea breeze.

The only thing that could have made it better was if it had been Saturday rather than Monday. The weekends meant more visitors to Buck Island, and more visitors meant more business, and Ellery was going to need more business—a lot more business—to keep the Crow's Nest sailing along. Seeing that Ronny had no interest in pitching *Night Chess* to anyone.

The scenes are void of meaningful or compelling conflict.

What did that even mean? Well, okay, Ellery knew what it meant, but he didn't like conflict. Not in his movies and not in real life.

Conflict arrives, is instantly resolved, and the narrative course continues unaffected.

Ellery muttered, "You say that like it's a bad thing."

The bells on the front door jingled merrily as Mrs. Nelson swept in. Ellery's heart sank.

Hermione Nelson was a heavyset woman in her late sixties with startlingly blue eyes, hair as red as a rusty battleship, and a small, pinched-looking mouth that gave the impression that the effort of keeping her thoughts to herself was starting to give her heartburn. Except, she never kept her thoughts to herself, so…

Mrs. Nelson was under the impression she was Ellery's best customer, and she would've been if she didn't return three quarters of everything she bought.

"Ellery, this book was a complete waste of my time. I can't believe you recommended it." Mrs. Nelson reached the wooden counter, fished around in her patchwork bag, and thrust a battered copy of *The Better Sister* by Alafair Burke at him.

"I'm sorry. It made pretty much everyone's Best Of lists for 2019." Ellery took the hardcover, wincing inwardly at the sight of folded page corners.

"I don't want to read about nasty people."

"Well, we're a mystery bookstore," Ellery pointed out. "Safe to say, at least one character in every book is going to be *kind of* nasty."

Mrs. Nelson was not amused. "I like my murders to happen to nice people. What about that new one from Joanne Fluke? I think I might like that."

"I'm not sure we have any copies le—"

Mrs. Nelson beamed. "I'll just go and check. We can do an even exchange. That will keep things simple for you."

Uh, no, actually that would complicate everything, but Mrs. Nelson was already bustling away, making a beeline for the Cozy Mystery section.

Ellery swallowed his exasperation. He was still trying to build his customer base—and being suspected of murder had not helped matters along—so he felt he had to be extra accommodating to the customers he did have, even if some of them were using him more as a library than a bookstore.

He gazed out the large bay windows at the people strolling past, ice-cream cones in one hand, shopping bags in the other. A former fishing village—actually, a former pirate sanctuary, if you wanted to go *way* back—Pirate's Cove was working hard to transform itself into a premium tourist destination. Things were pretty quiet in the fall, winter, and spring, but once summer arrived, the little windswept island offered biking, hiking, sailing, fishing, and lots of sunny beaches to explore.

The island also boasted two historic lighthouses: North Point and Half Moon Bay, as well as the partially buried ruins of a pirate fortress. Nearly half the island had been set aside for conservation, with the northwestern tip serving as a resting stop for birds migrating along the Atlantic flyway.

The potential for business was definitely there. The business itself...not so much. Not yet.

But the citizens of Pirate's Cove were working to change that, and no one was working harder than Ellery.

The Crow's Nest had been underwater when he'd inherited it from Great-great-great-aunt Eudora, and it was still leaking like a sieve, but the sight of all those ice-cream cones and shopping bags gave him hope.

Even better than ice cream and shopping bags was the sight of Police Chief Jack Carson heading toward the front door of the Crow's Nest. Jack's gaze met Ellery's through the glass, and Ellery's heart skipped a beat. He smiled. Jack smiled back.

Over the past weeks, he and Ellery had become friendly—which was not exactly the same thing as being friends, but they were moving in that direction. Ellery was happy. He liked Jack. He was also attracted to Jack—and he wasn't alone in that; most of the fairer sex of Pirate's Cove was attracted to the handsome, widowed chief of police. Jack was in his late thirties, a lean six-foot-nothing with sun-streaked brown hair and piercing green-blue eyes. He had a terrific smile, which he kept mostly in reserve. It was *because* Ellery was attracted to Jack that he was grateful their friendship was developing slowly, maybe even cautiously.

The fact was, he did not have good luck with relationships. Not romantic relationships. So, thinking of Jack as strictly friends took the pressure off.

At least that's what Ellery told himself.

The bell offered a silvery welcome as Jack stepped inside the Crow's Nest.

"Why, howdy, Sheriff," Ellery drawled in his best minor-character-in-a-made-for-TV-Western accent.

"Why, howdy, Mr. Page," Jack drawled back, and maybe it was being from California, but he did that *Home on the Range* accent better than Ellery, who even had three minor second-cowpoke-from-the-left credits on his acting résumé.

Good intentions notwithstanding, something about Jack's deep, pleasant voice always gave Ellery a little tingle at the base of his spine. It was distracting, to say the least.

"T'warn't fixin' to see you quite so soon."

Jack grimaced and dropped the drawl. "I know. I have to take a rain check on lunch. Emergency town-council meeting."

"*Oh.*" Ellery didn't bother to hide his disappointment. He and Jack had lunch together about once a week. Jack had also twice come out to Captain's Seat, the falling-down 18th Century mansion Ellery had inherited, to help with renovations. "That's too bad. What's the emergency?"

"The lack of any game plan to handle the media once they arrive for the trial."

"Ugh. Right."

Ellery's recent experience with the editor of the *Scuttlebutt Weekly* had left him with a sour taste in his mouth for members of the media.

"Yeah, anyway, I was wondering—" Jack broke off as Watson, the black spaniel-mix puppy Ellery had adopted, wandered out of his crate behind the counter to say hello. Jack squatted down. "Hey, you little rascal."

Watson threw himself on his back, wriggling in delight—which was the typical reaction of most Pirate's Cove citizens when Jack Carson appeared.

Sure enough...

"Oh! Chief Carson. I thought I recognized your voice." Mrs. Nelson came around the corner of tall bookshelves.

Jack rose. "Mrs. Nelson. How are you?"

Mrs. Nelson proceeded to tell him in detail.

Mrs. Smith—small and slender, with thinning sandy hair—appeared at the counter, a stack of used paperbacks from the bargain bin in hand, and beamed at Ellery. "Ring these up, dear." She turned immediately to Jack. "Chief Carson, how is the Maples case coming along?" Mrs. Smith was a devoted viewer of the Investigation Discovery channel and believed herself to be an expert in criminal investigations.

"We're gathering evidence and building our case, Mrs. Smith," Jack said politely.

"The circumstantial evidence alone ought to be enough to secure a conviction."

"I prefer direct evidence." Jack glanced at Ellery, and Ellery grimaced. There had been plenty of circumstantial evidence against him in the Maples case, but luckily Jack had dug deeper.

Mrs. Nelson, who had not finished detailing the delights of her gallbladder surgery, cut in. "Call me old-fashioned, but I don't trust a doctor younger than my grandchildren."

"Isn't your youngest grandchild around eight years old?" Jack inquired.

Mrs. Nelson ignored that.

"I always suspected there was something up with that man," said Mrs. Ferris, materializing out of the brand-new True Crime section, to join in the conversation. "His taste in sports coats was a clear indicator of a deranged psyche."

"Juries *like* circumstantial evidence," Mrs. Smith insisted.

Watson, wearying of so many conversations that had nothing to do with how adorable he was, waddled toward the front door. Ellery dashed around the counter to scoop him up as two young women opened the door, saw the crowd at the counter, and ducked back out.

He sighed, glanced back at the huddle in front of the cash register, and caught Jack's gaze. Jack looked resigned, as well as...something else. Ellery didn't know him well enough to interpret his every expression, but he had the impression Jack had been about to ask him something.

Well, whatever it was, it would have to wait. Jack's fan club was not going anywhere soon.

Ellery returned Watson to his crate, gave him a chew toy, and began to ring up Mrs. Smith's books. He listened with half an ear to the conversation around him. He was surprised Jack had not already extricated himself and escaped, something he was very good at in such situations.

He looked up, feeling Jack's gaze, and they smiled at each other again. It warmed Ellery. He really did like Jack. He liked his easy, straightforward manner. Nothing ever seemed to fluster Jack. He liked the way he was with Watson. He liked how Jack looked—broad shoulders and narrow hips, muscular arms and long legs—in his trim navy-blue uniform. He liked the way Jack's smile formed little crinkles around the corners of his eyes.

Jack started to speak, but Mr. Starling appeared at the counter with Lee Child's latest. "Ellery, my boy, could you tell me the price of this book?"

Ellery was about to rattle off the price, which happened to be clearly labeled on a sticker on the back of the book, when Mr. Starling turned to Jack.

"Chief Carson, I didn't see you there!"

Ellery resisted the urge to roll his eyes.

"Morning, Mr. Starling." Jack glanced instinctively at the door, and Ellery bit back a grin. Everyone had their breaking point, and Mr. Starling was usually it.

"Nice day today, eh, Chief?"

"Yep."

Ellery handed the receipt with the stack of paperbacks to Mrs. Smith, who dumped everything in her canvas shopping bag. She turned to Mr. Starling. "How's your wife, Stanley?"

Mr. Starling waved dismissively. "Doing fine, I suppose. Spends her days staring at the boob tube."

Mrs. Nelson began, "I don't believe televisions still have tubes—"

Mr. Starling ignored her. "Chief, I've meaning to talk to you about those young hooligans hanging out on the beach every evening. It wouldn't surprise me if they were doing drugs and whatnot."

"Sure," Jack said, edging toward the door. "Why don't you come down to the station later and have a chat with Officer Martin."

"I'm not sure young Martin is old enough to know what's what."

Mrs. Smith was also angling toward the door with Jack and Mr. Starling. "Lovely visiting with you all, but I must pick up some scallops from Finn's."

Ellery opened his mouth, but Mrs. Nelson was there before him.

"You've forgotten to pay, Jane."

Mrs. Smith looked startled and then laughed gaily. "Oh dear. I'm always doing that!"

Yes, she was, but Ellery chuckled too. Politely.

Jack said mildly, "Uh-oh, Mrs. Smith. Should I save space for your mug shot on the station bulletin board?"

Mrs. Smith turned red. Her laugh sounded a little hysterical that time. The others joined in. She hurriedly dug her pocketbook out and handed over a twenty-dollar bill. "Keep the change, dear."

In fact, she was twenty-three cents short, but Ellery knew to choose his battles. "Thanks, Mrs. Smith."

The shop door flew open, the bell clanging wildly, and Nora Sweeny rushed in, narrowly missing colliding with Jack and his entourage.

"Ellery, dearie! So sorry I'm late, but you won't believe what's happened!"

Nora was Ellery's shop assistant. She was about seventy, small but mighty. In spirit, at least. Her hair was gray, her eyes were gray, but her personality was bright and cheerful as the gold and blue city flag she had helped design. Once upon a time, Nora had been president of the Pirate's Cove Historical Society, and it was her life's ambition to bring that now defunct organization back to life.

"What's happened?" Ellery and everyone else in the Crow's Nest chorused.

Nora skidded to a stop, looking nonplussed. "I didn't realize—well, the news is bound to be all over the village by now. I still can't believe it. It's a...a *calamity*."

"What's a calamity?" Jack, being in the calamity business, was frowning.

"Skull House has been sold!"

"Isn't that good news?" Ellery was confused. "I thought the historical society was planning to buy it for their new home base." It was pretty much all Nora had been talking about for the last two weeks, ever since the news broke that Skull House was going on the market.

"But that's just it. It's not us. The Historical Society *hasn't* purchased the house. We were outbid. We didn't even know we *were* bidding. Someone—an outsider—swooped in at the last moment and stole the house out from under us!" Nora reached the counter, resting her elbows on it and dropping her head in her hands.

Ellery bent over her. "Are you all right?"

Nora, still clutching her head, shook no.

Everyone else—with the exception of Jack—was talking at once: *who, what, where, when, why...*

The *why* was the real question, in Ellery's opinion. Why anyone, let alone the Pirate's Cove Historical Society, would want to buy Skull House, was a mystery to him. For one thing, it was out on Pequot Bluffs, miles from the village. For another, the house was a wreck. Not as much of a wreck as Captain's Seat, maybe—or maybe it was, because no one had lived there for the last fifty years. That amount of dust was probably lethal.

"I'm sorry. But, you know, maybe it's for the best," Ellery said. "Skull House would probably cost a fortune to get in shape, and it isn't exactly conveniently located. There are other houses."

"No, there really aren't," Mrs. Nelson informed him. "When was the last time you saw property for sale on the island?"

Well…never. Granted, he had only lived on Buck Island for four months.

"And no new construction," Mr. Starling said. "Per the Buck Island Conservancy."

"The Maples' properties are going to come on the market eventually."

"Eventually," agreed Mrs. Nelson. "Which could be years from now. You know how courts are."

Nora moaned. "*I* know! I know *all* that."

The bells on the door chimed softly as Jack eased it open. He raised a hand in farewell to Ellery, who nodded back regretfully. He couldn't blame Jack for making his escape. He just wished Jack had taken the others with him.

"To think an outsider could just come in and buy one of our historical landmarks." That was Mrs. Ferris.

"It's not actually a landmark, is it?" Ellery asked. "Not technically. Not legally."

No one bothered to reply.

Mrs. Smith asked, "Who *is* this mysterious outsider? Who has bought Skull House?"

Nora raised her head. Her eyes were dry, so that was good. In fact, she looked more mad than sad.

"He's a writer. Very popular, if you like *that* kind of thing."

"What kind of thing?" Ellery asked. If this mysterious someone was a mystery writer, this might not be a total disaster. It was very hard to get authors to appear for book signings when they had to travel by ferry to a small island in the middle of nowhere. Okay, Rhode Island. Still.

"Sex?" Mr. Starling asked hopefully.

Nora said in tones of loathing, "I'm speaking of Brandon Abbott."

Ellery stared at her. "Brandon?" he repeated. "Brandon Abbott?" He heard and understood the words, but somehow they seemed to have short-circuited his brain.

"Brandon Abbott. Yes." Nora's gaze grew curious at his obvious shock.

"I know him!" Mrs. Smith exclaimed. "He's like Stephen King. He writes all that spooky stuff."

"Horror," Ellery said, which pretty much summed up his feelings regarding Brandon Abbott.

"Do you *know* Brandon Abbott?" Mrs. Nelson asked, surprised.

"I used to. He's my ex."

"I thought—" objected Nora.

"My *other* ex," Ellery said.

CHAPTER TWO

The familiar, comforting, theatrical scents of aged wood, fabric, mothballs, and sewing-machine oil greeted Ellery as he walked into the costume room at the old theater on Wallace Street Monday evening. It was clear, from the sudden cease fire, that everyone had been talking about him. Even the blank papier-mâché faces of the masks on the prop shelf looked vaguely guilty.

Nora, in charge of costumes for the play, glanced up from her worktable beneath the fluorescent lights and audibly gulped. "Dearie! There you are! We were just wondering whether you'd make tonight's rehearsal."

"Why wouldn't I?" Ellery asked.

"Oh, well, you know…" Nora faltered. "You've got little Watson to consider."

"Little Watson is being babysat—puppy-sat—by Sandy's daughter. Like he's been every other rehearsal night."

Nora cleared her throat nervously. "True. True. That child is wonderful with animals."

Ellery shook his head.

The Scallywags, Pirate's Cove's local amateur theater guild, were putting on *Murder Mansion*, which Ellery had been talked into adapting from his own rejected screenplay *Murder Under the Eaves*. He was serving as a consultant to the production.

His gaze traveled over the little crowd, taking in the uncomfortable expressions of nineteen-year-old Libby Tulley and her boyfriend, Felix Jones, son of Pirate's Cove newly reelected Mayor Cyrus Jones, who was also present, Nan Sweeny, Sue Lewis (oh, great, the editor of the *Scuttlebutt Weekly* was part of this gossip session), and a few others, including theater director Dylan Carter.

In addition to running the theater, Dylan owned the Toy Chest, the shop next door to the Crow's Nest. Dylan was the closest thing Ellery had to a best friend in Pirate's Cove. During the rainy winter months they had bonded over a shared love of Broadway, "real" pizza, flavored vodka, and cities that did not roll up the sidewalks at nine thirty.

"*Et tu, Brute*?" Ellery said.

Dylan blushed. "Hey, I'm here for a fitting!"

"Turns out so am I!" He wasn't even sure what he meant by that, but everyone laughed.

Everyone but Dylan, who looked pained.

Libby giggled. "Not me. I want to hear all the news."

"Quiet, you," Dylan growled. He was small, slim, and always impeccably dressed—in costume or out. A well-preserved sixty-something, he had merry blue eyes and silver hair stylishly buzzed short on one side. When they'd first met, Ellery had figured Dylan was gay, which just went to show you should never judge a book—or a theater director—by its cover.

Libby laughed again, unimpressed.

Anyway, it wasn't like Ellery wasn't used to it. You can't be suspected of murder and not spark a little neighborly chitchat. But after the Maples murder case wrapped up, he'd hoped his fellow citizens would find somebody else to talk about. And, in fairness, they had: Brandon Abbott. But Ellery had made a fatal mistake when he'd blurted that shocked admission in front of five of Pirate's Cove's finest blabbermouths, about once having been close to Brandon. Brandon was the nearest thing to a celebrity resident Buck Island had ever had.

It was probably all over the island now—and half the island wasn't even inhabited.

"What's he like?" Felix asked. "Is he as creepy as his books?"

No question who *he* was.

"No clue. I haven't seen him in years," Ellery said.

And he'd have been happy to go more years without seeing Brandon. He knew it was paranoid to think he had anything to do with Brandon's decision to buy Skull House. Brandon probably hadn't given him a thought since they split up. Out of sight, out of mind was Brandon's motto. Especially when he owed you money.

"How did you meet him?" Libby asked.

Ellery sighed. "We were at Tisch together."

"Tisch?"

"The New York University Tisch School of the Arts. We were roommates."

"Okay, people!" Dylan clapped his hands. "Enough lollygagging. We've got four rehearsals left, and we need every minute."

He ushered his cast out of the costume room, throwing Ellery an apologetic look.

"And at your age!" Ellery said—only half joking—and Dylan—only half joking—glowered.

As the last cast member filed out, Nora cleared her throat. "I *may* owe one or two deposits to the, er, gossip jar."

Ellery snorted. "Ya think?"

"But no one said anything *bad* about you. Not even Sue Lewis. Well, not *really*. We all know what Sue's problem is. It's just…you're different. You're interesting. And Brandon Abbott is famous."

Ellery shook his head and exited stage left. He made his way through the backstage rabbit warren of dressing rooms and narrow hallways—passing gallery after gallery of framed photos of cast and productions through the decades—to the stairs and then to the front of the house. He found a seat a few rows back from the stage and settled down for the dubious honor of watching his words be brought to life.

Did the rehearsal go well?

Ellery had no idea. He found it difficult to concentrate, which was hopefully nothing to do with the play and everything to do with the roiling unease he'd felt since learning Brandon might eventually move to Pirate's Cove.

On the one hand, he really didn't believe Brandon's decision to move to Pirate's Cove could have anything to do with him. They had literally not spoken in years. On the other hand, it was a weird coincidence, made weirder by the fact that Brandon was not and had never been a small-town boy—and towns just didn't get any smaller than Pirate's Cove.

But maybe Brandon had changed.

They'd both had time to grow up. To realize there were more important things than career—and more important careers than acting. Brandon was a famous writer now. He was rich and well known. True, one of the things he was known for was being as peculiar as his books, but that was part shtick. Not that Brandon hadn't always been a little odd. A little unpredictable. A little…alarming.

The good news was Skull House was in a terrible state of disrepair, so it would be months, maybe even a year or more, before Brandon would be able to move in. Given his attention span, there was a fair chance he'd never come to Buck Island at all.

"Are you heading over to the Salty Dog?" Dylan called from the stage as the rehearsal broke up. "Can you grab us a table?"

"Yes. I'll see you there," Ellery called back, shrugging into his jacket.

Sue was standing next to Libby at the side exit. Her eyes, meeting Ellery's, seemed bright with glee, and he felt a prickle of apprehension. Sue was the editor-in-chief (not to mention owner) of Pirate's Cove's only newspaper, the *Scuttlebutt Weekly*. When Ellery had been the number-one suspect in the Maples murder, Sue had lambasted him in a series of editorials. In fact, she had all but called for a lynching.

True, the paper had issued a lukewarm apology once the true culprit had been identified, but Ellery was pretty sure Sue still saw him as a menace to society.

"I might organize an exclusive with him," Sue was saying to Libby. "Especially if he's writing a novel set right here in Pirate's Cove. You wouldn't mind, would you, Ellery?"

Ellery played dumb. "Wouldn't mind what?"

"Me scoring an interview with Brandon Abbott." Sue's gaze was challenging. She was just a little older than him. A petite and pretty pit bull of a woman. Her blonde hair was long and straight, her brown eyes wide and misleadingly soft, her makeup heavily influenced by J.Lo.

Ellery shrugged. "What's it to me? I haven't seen him in seven years."

"But you did use to be, um, partners, right?"

Ellery grinned. "Are you trying to interview me again, Sue?"

Libby laughed, and Sue's smile grew tight. "Just a courtesy check. The media has painted your boyfriend as a colorful character. I think it would be fun to interview him, seeing that we've finally got someone famous living in PICO."

That was probably supposed to be a dig at Ellery and his failed acting career. He didn't care what Sue thought, but it seemed others did. Nearly everyone on the island subscribed to the *Scuttlebutt Weekly.*

"I'm sure your subscribers would love it."

Sue's eyes narrowed; no doubt, she was suspecting Ellery of sarcasm. "You're not worried about what your ex might say about you?"

"Ter-ri-fied," Ellery drawled. He winked at Libby and pushed out through the exit door, stepping into the cool, damp night. He let the heavy door swing shut behind him.

* * * *

The first person Ellery spotted when he walked into the Salty Dog was Jack.

Partly that was because Jack was in his usual place—on the opposite side of the room from Ellery's usual place. Partly that was because he was sort of looking for Jack, even though he told himself not to look for Jack.

As always, the pub was doing a brisk trade, and Ellery worked his way through the crowd to the bar, requesting a table for the Scallywags. The nice thing about life in a small town was that instead of pub owner Tom Tulley falling over laughing, he tossed a towel over his arm and went to commandeer a long table in the center of the room for his regulars.

Ellery considered and then walked over to Jack's table. Jack, reading through a stack of papers, didn't glance up until Ellery said, "Hey, stranger."

Jack's head jerked up, and his serious expression relaxed into a smile. "Hey. Long time no see." As Ellery hesitated, he added, "Pull up a chair."

Ellery did so, admitting, "I didn't want to interrupt, if you're working."

Jack was pretty much always working.

Jack offered one of those crinkly, unexpectedly engaging grins. "Just going over some case notes. You can interrupt me anytime."

Well, no. And Jack had no qualms speaking up when it was not a good time. Really, that was part of what Ellery liked about him. He was direct and straightforward. It was refreshing after Todd. Actually, it was refreshing after Brandon too. Come to think of it, there had been a real lack of direct and straightforward romantic interests in Ellery's life.

Not that—despite a bit of flirtation—Jack was exactly a romantic interest. It was kind of hard to define their relationship. Friends with possibilities?

"Did rehearsal just wind up?" Jack asked.

Ellery nodded. He smiled thanks as Reg, the bartender, brought him his usual Upside-Down Pirate martini. As he sipped the zingy blue cocktail, he considered whether this was a good time to mention Brandon. It felt weird not to mention something that was so much on his mind, but at the same time, was it liable to seem like he thought his former relationship would have some special importance for Jack? It's not like they were dating.

Jack asked, "Are you enjoying seeing your play being acted out on the stage?"

"Well… I mean, yes. It's flattering Dylan thought it was good enough to produce. But also, it's kind of cringy."

Jack's brows rose. "Cringy?"

"Yes. Lines that read fine on the page are different when they're spoken aloud. Sometimes they're better. But sometimes…"

Jack seemed to give Ellery's words serious consideration. "You think maybe it's the acting? The Scallywags are amateurs, after all."

"Sometimes it's the acting, for sure." Ellery could say that, being a former actor with no illusions as to his own limited ability. His career, such as it was, had been largely based on the fact that he was easy to get along with and had been blessed with physical fitness and symmetrical bone structure. He knew how to smile, and he knew how to look terrified. That was pretty much his dramatic range. And it hadn't always been acting.

Jack said, "I'm sure people will enjoy the play."

"I hope so. It seemed to go fine tonight." He added carefully, "Well, except for all the talk about my ex buying Skull House."

Jack had been reaching for his beer. He sloshed a little on the table, glancing quickly at Ellery. "*Todd* bought Skull House?"

"No, no. My other ex. My first ex."

"Er, how many exes do you *have* exactly?" Jack inquired.

"Wellll, you know."

"Nope."

"It's just that I had an active social life before I moved to Pirate's Cove."

"I don't doubt it."

Ellery laughed at Jack's rueful expression. "Two. Only two what I'd call *serious* relationships in my life. And I wouldn't call Brandon serious so much as…"

"As…?"

"Significant."

"Ah."

"Brandon taught me everything I did *not* want in a relationship." Ellery wasn't kidding about that. "I'm not looking forward to his moving here. But maybe he's not planning to live on the island. Maybe he bought the place as an investment."

"An investment? Skull House? He must need one heck of a tax deduction." Jack swallowed a mouthful of beer, studying Ellery. "So there's bad blood between you and—"

Before Ellery could respond, the door to the pub was shoved open as the Scallywags arrived on a breath of chilly night air. Everyone seemed to be talking at once as they flung off their coats and scarves, calling for drinks. The already busy pub grew instantly louder and more boisterous.

"I guess that's my cue." Ellery smiled, pushing back his chair.

Jack seemed about to say something, but instead smiled back. "Enjoy your evening."

"You too." Ellery picked up his drink and moved to join the cast and crew crowding around the long table in the center of the room.

"There you are. The man of the hour," Dylan greeted him, scraping his chair sideways to make room for Ellery's.

Ellery laughed and shook his head at what was clearly Dylan trying to make up for earlier. He couldn't help wishing Jack had asked him to stay. He knew he wasn't imagining that spark between them. There was definitely more than just liking and friendship going on between them; it wasn't all on his side.

He glanced over, and Jack was once more reading his file.

"Ellery, do you think Brandon Abbott is going to write his next book about Skull House?" Sue called.

Honestly. Brandon. *Again?* Was there no other news on this island?

"Like I said earlier, I haven't spoken to him in years," Ellery replied. Which was true, but even if he'd had a definitive answer, he'd have kept it to himself. He'd learned the hard way that for Sue, nothing was off the record.

Cyrus Jones, balding and portly with warm brown eyes and—usually—a wide smile, exclaimed, "Surely not!" He sounded genuinely shocked. As Pirate's Cove's mayor, he was always fretting about what might reflect badly on the village.

The others were amused.

"Maybe he came here because he wants you back," Libby interjected. "That would be *so* romantic."

"God, I hope not!" Ellery shuddered visibly, which got a bigger laugh.

"Then we can assume your relationship didn't end well?" Sue inquired.

Ellery hung on to his smile, but Sue was seriously starting to get on his nerves. He turned to Cyrus, who was sitting on his left. "Is there some reason someone would want to write about Skull House?"

Was it his imagination, or did the mayor hesitate? "I'm afraid I'm just as in the dark as everyone else," Cyrus said. "People don't need the mayor's permission to buy property."

"Isn't it supposed to be haunted or something?"

"Ghosts!" Cyrus shook his head at the idea.

Dylan's brows rose. "You haven't heard the legends?"

"I've heard the building is unsafe."

"It *is* unsafe," Cyrus said. "It should have been razed to the ground years ago."

Nora gasped in protest.

Felix groaned, "Jeez. It's a historical landmark, Dad."

"No, it certainly is not. It's just old and dangerous."

Dylan said, "It's one of the oldest houses on the island—"

"It's cursed!" Libby said eagerly, and Felix laughed at her. "It is," she protested. "That's the legend."

Nora, ever the island historian, chimed in. "Skull House was built by John Mansfield in 1608. It's not a historical landmark. Not yet. But the property *is* of significant cultural and historical interest. It's a disgrace that it's fallen into the hands of a private party."

"Who was John Mansfield?" Ellery tried to head Nora off before she could get too wound up.

Dylan grinned. "The original pirate of Pirate's Cove."

"Seriously?"

Dylan bobbed his head side to side. "Well, *one* of the original pirates. One of the big guns. Pun intended."

Ellery nodded. He was aware that Rhode Island—and Buck Island in particular—had an impressive piratical history. In fact, Rhode Island itself had been discovered by a pirate, named by a pirate, and kept afloat—in a manner of speaking—by pirates. Not that it was all love and kisses between the Ocean State and her founders. In July 1723, twenty-six pirates had been hung in one day in Newport.

"Buck Island used to be known as the Port Royal of the New World until people like your own ancestor Captain Horatio Page made it their home port."

"And John Mansfield was one of these pirates?"

"Yep. One of the worst. Right alongside Edward Low and Edward Teach. He was cruel and ruthless, although according to historical accounts, he was also handsome and could be very charming. Nowadays we'd probably call him a sociopath. Back then he was just part of the scourge… Anyway, he fancied himself a ladies' man, and used to, er, appropriate the female slaves of vessels he commandeered. Occasionally he even brought them back to New England. The women, I mean."

"Yikes."

"*Appropriate?* You can say rape," Nora put in tartly. "We're all adults here. Let's not romanticize the past."

Dylan nodded in acknowledgment. "According to the story, Mansfield became obsessed with a local girl named Ann Rathbone. She wasn't having any of it, so he kidnapped her and carried her off to Skull House. I don't know why he thought he could get away with that. There were a lot of things the town fathers could turn a blind eye to, but abducting 'a lady of prudent virtue' wasn't one of them. Mansfield did it nonetheless. We can all use our imagination as to what happened next—or Nora can spell it out for us."

Nora sniffed in disapproval.

"The story goes, once Mansfield fell asleep, Ann stabbed him with his own dagger. Unfortunately, instead of hanging around for the medal she was no doubt due, she followed time-honored tradition and cursed the house and all who dwelt within, and promptly jumped into the sea."

"Now there's a cozy bedtime story." Ellery spoke lightly, but he was genuinely horrified. Sure, it sounded like a fairy tale, and even if it was true, it had all happened centuries ago, but it was too easy to imagine how terrifying that poor tortured girl's final night had been. She had been as real in her moment as they were in theirs.

"Alas, the real Pirates of the Caribbean weren't nearly as charming as their film counterparts," Dylan said.

"So who haunts Skull House? Ann Rathbone or John Mansfield?"

"Oh no. That's—" Nora began, but then, uncharacteristically, stopped.

A funny silence followed. Ellery glanced around the table, but the Scallywags seemed to be studying the pub menu like it contained the secrets of the universe.

"Who needs a drink?" Dylan asked, rising. Everyone began to call out orders.

Ellery was thinking that Dylan's story offered an explanation as to why Brandon might develop an interest in living in a potentially haunted house on a tiny island off the coast of Rhode Island. He always based his novels on real-life crimes. Of course, in his books, the reasons for the crimes were ultimately supernatural. In Brandon's world, ninety percent of homicides were committed by disgruntled witches and displaced demons. Skull House, with its grim and gruesome legend, was probably ideal for Brandon's purposes. Although choosing to live there seemed a *little* extreme.

Maybe it was the writer's version of method acting.

"Ellery? Another?" Dylan prompted.

Did he want another? It was late. The drive home to Captain's Seat was relatively short, but the country lanes were dark and occasionally dangerous. Wildlife—and even dogs—had been known to pop out of nowhere.

"I'm okay," he said.

"Do you think you could introduce us to him?" Libby asked, jarring Ellery out of his reflections.

"Who *me*?" It was hard to think of anything he would *less* like to do.

He was about to tell Libby so, when the door to the pub seemed to blow open on a gust of salt-laced night air. Everyone at the table—in fact, the very room—seemed to give a collective start, as though

Dylan's story of the bloodstained past had rattled their nerves just a tiny bit.

As Ellery turned, he noticed Jack appraising the new arrival with cool, considering eyes.

His heart sank. Somehow, he just knew... He looked toward the door, and yep, sure enough, there he was. Never one to miss making an entrance.

Brandon.

CHAPTER THREE

If there was one thing Brandon had always enjoyed, it was attention. That did not seem to have changed over the years.

Tall and lean, with longish black hair and a narrow, pale face, he surveyed the room for a moment. Then…

"Goooood eeeeeevening!" he called. "*I am Count Dracoola.*"

You could have heard a pin drop in the astonished silence that followed.

Count Dracula? Seriously? And yet, instead of getting a pie in the face or, at the very least, a community cold shoulder, a bunch of people burst out laughing, jumped up and crowded round, asking for his autograph.

Sue Lewis actually hopped out of her chair and muscled in, introducing herself and asking for an interview.

Un. Be. Lievable.

It was like they thought Brandon was someone famous. Okay, he *was* famous, but not so famous he typically got mobbed. Unless things had changed a lot over the years.

Maybe they had, because the good folks of Pirate's Cove were fawning over him as if Stephen King had come to town. Mayor Jones was pumping Brandon's hand like he thought he was going to start spouting golden coins. And those who hadn't joined the welcoming committee were whispering to each other and watching the show like it *was* a show.

Well, not everybody.

Nora was glaring at the burbling, babbling circle around Brandon with such naked dislike, Ellery felt uncomfortable.

Did Skull House really matter that much to her?

And Jack...

Ellery glanced at Jack again, and felt his face warm. Jack was looking at him. As their gazes met, Jack smiled quizzically. Ellery rolled his eyes. He felt instantly better, though he wasn't sure why.

And the feeling didn't last long.

"Ellery!" Brandon cried, like a shipwrecked sailor spotting land.

Oh God. Ellery almost knocked his chair over as he tried to retreat from Brandon's rush to embrace him.

"I can't believe it's really you! When I saw you'd been arrested for murder..."

"I wasn't arrested," Ellery protested.

"He should have been," Sue put in. Meeting Ellery's gaze, she laughed. "Kidding!"

Yeah, not so much.

Brandon said, "The police in this town must be idiots!"

Ellery couldn't help an instinctive look at Jack, who was considering Brandon with narrowed eyes.

"There was a lot of circumstantial evidence," Ellery offered lamely.

"There certainly was," Sue said. "Mr. Abbott—"

Brandon ignored her, still gazing at Ellery in what was surely exaggerated wonder. "El, you look *terrific*. I can't get over it. I mean, you were always gorgeous, but you've finally grown into that nose."

That was classic Brandon. The over-the-top compliment followed by the laughing smackdown.

"Uh, thanks," Ellery said. "You look good too."

It was faint praise, and Brandon seemed to acknowledge it with a rueful grin. The truth was, he *did* look good. He still favored unredeemed black, but these days his clothes were expensive and well-cut. He had filled out a bit too, so he appeared lean and fit versus cadaverous. He was still pale, but he'd had his brows micro-bladed and his lashes tinted, so his ebony eyes stood out in dramatic contrast to the rest of his narrow, rather ascetic features. Also, his stick-straight black hair had been cut by someone who knew what they were doing. It made a difference.

All in all, he looked well-groomed and affluent. He looked confident.

"Aren't you going to introduce me to your friends and my future neighbors?" Brandon asked.

"Sure," Ellery said, and began to make introductions, up and down the long table. It was probably petty to be irritated by the way everyone fell over themselves to meet Brandon. After all, he *was* kind of a big deal these days. It was just that Ellery had never realized how many fans of horror fiction apparently lived on the island.

"Are you really going to live in Skull House, Mr. Abbott?" Libby asked.

"Of course. That's the idea," Brandon said. "Although I may hit up my old roommate for lodging during the renovation phase." He smiled at Ellery.

"*What?*" Ellery didn't try to hide his alarm.

"It'll be like old times," Brandon said. "Man, we used to laugh together."

True. They had some good times. Especially in college. But Brandon had not adjusted well to adulting. Clearly, he'd overcome some obstacles, but the idea of any kind of second act with Brandon was an absolute nonstarter for Ellery.

Ellery said quickly, "I wish. But unfortunately, there was a fire at Captain's Seat a couple of weeks ago, so a lot of the house is unlivable."

That was a complete exaggeration. Yes, there had been a fire, and yes, there was a fair bit of damage—mostly smoke damage—on the second floor, but the house had six bedrooms and seven baths.

There was still plenty of inhabitable floor space in the old mansion.

"I'm not picky. I can bunk down anywhere."

"Yeah. No," Ellery said, and meant it.

"Something can certainly be arranged," Cyrus said quickly. "Won't you sit down and join us, Mr. Abbott?"

"There's plenty of room at the inn," Nan Sweeny chirped. Nan was Nora's niece. She owned the Seacrest Inn.

"Thank you for the suggestion," Brandon told her, taking the seat Cyrus had abandoned for him at the crowded table. That put him right next to Ellery, his knee nudging Ellery's, his elbow brushing Ellery's. "That's always a possibility." He was giving Ellery a sideways look that managed to mix reproach with mockery. Brandon knew perfectly well Ellery would still have been coming up with excuses even if *he'd* owned the Seacrest Inn and not the slightly scorched Captain's Seat.

Felix leaned across the table. "Mr. Abbott, are you going to write your next book about Skull House?"

Was it Ellery's imagination, or was there something odd in the brief lull that followed the mayor's son's question?

"Definitely," Brandon replied. "I paid top dollar for those legends, and I intend to get my money's worth."

Everyone laughed, but again, Ellery thought there was something uneasy in the sound.

"I should be going." Nora rose, dragging on her black wool coat. The evenings were still quite chilly even in late spring.

"Oh, don't go," Brandon objected. "This is turning into a regular little Welcome Home party. How about another round of drinks? Totally on me!"

Libby, who frequently helped out in her father's pub, jumped up and began to take drink orders. Brandon looked around the pub with his glinting, black gaze as everyone applauded.

Everyone but Nora. She finished buttoning her coat and said in a clear, carrying voice, "However, this is not your home, Mr. Abbott. It never will be. You should think about taking Nan up on her offer."

"*Nora!*" Several people at the table made shushing motions.

Nora ignored them. "Skull House is not safe. And I'm not talking about the mold or the rotting floors or the rats." Her voice wobbled with emotion. "Not the four-footed kind!"

What the heck did that mean?

An uncomfortable pause followed her stark pronouncement.

"Now, now," Cyrus said quickly. "Mr. Abbott purchased the property. He can do what he likes with it, Nora."

Sue said, "Don't be a bad sport, Nora."

"Am I missing something?" Brandon murmured to Ellery.

Ellery didn't bother replying. He thought they both might be missing something.

Nora said, "When you get to be my age, you'll understand there are some things that shouldn't be tampered with. Things that are best left alone."

"You're wonderful. I'm going to put you in a book." Brandon chuckled, glancing around the table for approval. He didn't get it; everyone looked more ill at ease.

"Come on now, Nora," Dylan said kindly. "If the historical society had purchased Skull House, you'd have done plenty of tampering. Let's be fair about this."

Nora drew herself up to her full five feet, which, granted, wasn't terribly impressive. "Skull House is cursed," she pronounced. "No human can live there and thrive."

"It sounds perfect," Brandon retorted. "I prefer ghosts to humans anyway."

If he thought he was getting the last word, he didn't know Nora.

"Mark my words." Nora turned and strode from the pub, leaving a startled silence in her wake.

"Did she just say 'mark my words'?" Brandon was grinning, and the quick laughter of those still at the table held a note of relief.

Dylan said softly to Ellery, "Sometimes I think Nora really is a witch."

"I know." Ellery glanced over at Jack. He was speaking to Libby, and seemed to be declining the offer of a free drink.

"I should be going too," Ellery said. "Sandy's daughter must be in bed by now. I don't want Sandy to get stuck watching Watson."

"Watson's fine," Dylan said. "He'll be sound asleep."

That was probably true, but Ellery was more than ready to leave. It was late, and he was a little unsettled by Brandon's sudden appearance. It wasn't that he was still attracted to his former boyfriend, but Brandon was like a toothache. Hard to tune out. Ellery kept comparing the old Brandon with this new Brandon, which meant he kept remembering things he didn't want to think about. He did not want or need the distraction Brandon presented.

Unlike the rest of Pirate's Cove.

Wryly, he studied Brandon holding court at the table. The way people were acting, you'd have thought Johnny Depp was sitting there. Even Sue was pink-cheeked and eager as she filled him in on whatever it was she was gushing about. Ellery got it. Brandon was shiny and new, something folks in Pirate's Cove loved because there was so little of it. He couldn't blame them, but that didn't stop him from being a little disappointed that a free drink was enough to win everyone over.

"Are you really not going to invite me to stay with you?" Brandon asked suddenly. "Your oldest friend?"

Ellery snapped out of his preoccupation. He was uncomfortably aware that once again everyone at the table—maybe the entire pub—was staring their way.

"I explained why I can't have guests right now." He couldn't help adding, "And you're not my oldest friend. We haven't even seen each other in nearly a decade."

"That was your choice." Brandon had become a master of smiling blandly as he said embarrassing things. "And after everything I did for your career."

"My career is bookseller, and I owe it all to my Great-great-great-aunt Eudora."

"Your *real* career," Brandon insisted. "Your acting career." He turned to the others. "I wrote the part of Noah Street specifically for Ellery."

Why? Why? Why?

What had he done to deserve this?

"Noah Street..." Dylan mused. "Why is that name familiar?"

"I am a *bookseller*," Ellery insisted. "I sell books. All that-that other stuff is way behind me."

"Behind you or *beneath* you?" Brandon was still smiling, but Ellery knew those tight lips and narrowed eyes meant he was deeply miffed. "I see how it is. You're ashamed now. But you weren't too ashamed to run to the bank with all that money I made you."

"Were you a porn star?" Dylan was beaming, apparently delighted at the idea.

"Oh. My. GOD." Sue was bright-eyed and grinning, no doubt visualizing the next day's headlines.

"*No!*" Ellery glared at Brandon. "I certainly was not!"

"You seem to think you were prostituting your talent," Brandon said.

"Wait a minute," Felix said slowly. "Noah Street. I know that name…"

"Thanks a lot," Ellery told Brandon.

Brandon's smile was smug. "You're welcome."

"I *thought* you looked familiar. You were in all those *Happy Halloween! You're Dead* movies!"

Ellery groaned, instantly reprising several highlights of his greatest role.

"Dude, those flicks are *classic*!"

"I thought it was Elliot Parker who played Noah," Libby objected.

"*He's* Elliot Parker. Look at him!"

Every pair of eyes in the pub seemed trained on Ellery.

"Oh-kay." Ellery rose, grabbing his jacket. "It's late, and I've got an early start tomorrow. Great rehearsal, everyone. See you next time."

He fled, closing his ears to the laughter and clapping and calls for him to stay and have another drink.

* * * * *

"Ellery!"

A couple of yards down the street from the Salty Dog, Ellery stopped and looked back. To his surprise, Jack strode after him, his long shadow stretching like a hand across the cobblestones. His eyes gleamed, and his hair looked almost silver in the lamplight.

Ignoring his heart's happy jump, Ellery shoved his hands in the pockets of his jacket, waiting until Jack caught up to him.

He was braced for, well, he wasn't sure what. Anything from a pep talk to interrogation, but when Jack reached him, all he said was, "I thought I'd walk back with you to your car."

Ellery shrugged. "Sure." He gave Jack a sideways look. "This village *is* pretty dangerous at night."

Jack made a sound that fell somewhere between laugh and snort. "That's why they pay me the big bucks."

"*Do* they pay you big bucks?"

Jack laughed at the idea but said, "I'm not complaining."

They headed in the direction of the Crow's Nest, neither of them saying much at first.

The night air was moist—it was always damp by the sea—and ghostly mist rose from the cobblestones. Ellery was reminded of Nora's warning to Brandon. To be honest, it had sounded more like a threat than a warning. He'd known Nora was bitterly disappointed over the historical society losing Skull House to Brandon, but her behavior that evening left him feeling uneasy.

"Your friend Abbott is a piece of work," Jack observed finally.

Ellery groaned. "For the record, I was never a porn star."

"I know that." Jack sounded amused.

"I'm not sure everyone else does."

"I wouldn't worry about it."

Maybe Jack had missed the predatory gleam in Sue Lewis's gaze. Ellery hadn't. He insisted, "They were slasher movies, that's all."

Jack said, "When we were looking at you as a possible suspect in Trevor's murder, I went over your background thoroughly. I know about the Elliot Parker stage name. I can't say I ever saw any of your films."

"That's a blessing for both of us."

Jack laughed. A warm sound on a cold night. "They can't be that bad."

"Oh yes they can. They really can."

Jack laughed again, and Ellery thought how much he liked the sound.

They continued down the narrow street, past tall buildings, some with high mansard roofs, some with gabled roofs, all seeming more shadow than substance in the moonlight. It seemed strange to think that a few of these structures would have been standing back when John Mansfield had first laid eyes on poor Ann Rathbone.

Ellery said, "Brandon was always a weird mix of arrogance and massive insecurity. We did have some good times together, though."

"You had no idea he was moving to Pirate's Cove?"

"No way." He said curiously, "Did I *look* like I had any idea?"

"No," Jack admitted.

"I found out this morning. I thought it would be months before he showed up, if he ever did. I still can't understand it. He's the last person who would willingly choose to live on an island, let alone on an island in a dilapidated mansion, miles from the nearest town. He's a born and bred New Yorker. He loved the city. I can't imagine him living anywhere else."

"People change."

"True." Ellery had certainly changed. There had been a time when it would have been as unthinkable for him to move to a small island as he believed it was for Brandon.

They turned onto Main Street, and the harbor was before them: the starlit glitter of black water, the vague outline of boats, the ghostly rustle of sails and pennants. The moon hung in the sky like a crooked scythe.

"It's hard to keep secrets in a small town," Jack said.

"I don't know. For all the gossip, I sometimes get the feeling everyone in the village knows something I don't."

"Sure, when it comes to the small stuff..." Jack did not finish the thought, and Ellery wondered if he had been thinking aloud.

By then they had reached the parking area behind the Crow's Nest. Ellery's navy VW looked like a large black snail in the wan moonlight.

"Have you had the dashboard wiring checked out yet?" Jack asked. Not for the first time.

"I haven't had a chance." Ellery jingled his keys in his pocket. "It seems to be working okay again."

Jack opened his mouth, and to forestall a lecture, Ellery said, "Well, thanks for the company."

"Yeah." Jack sounded absent. His face was unreadable in the uncertain light. He said, "Ellery, would you—"

At the same moment, Ellery said, "Okay, then—"

They both stopped.

"Sorry," Jack said. "Go ahead."

Belatedly, Ellery realized what was happening. Excitement bloomed in his chest. He said quickly, "No, I was just... What were you saying?"

"Would you like to have dinner one night?" Jack sounded brusque. Maybe that was how he handled being nervous? Although it was hard to picture Jack nervous about anything, let alone grabbing a meal together.

And yet Ellery also felt unexpectedly nervous as he answered, "Sure. When?"

"I'd suggest Saturday night, but you've got the play. How about Wednesday?"

"Wednesday would be great." Sudden doubt assailed Ellery. Was Jack asking him out on a date, or was this just the p.m. equivalent of their lunchtime get-togethers? He said, "Is this a date or…" He added hastily, "Either is fine, of course."

"A date." Jack seemed to clip the words off.

"*Really?*" Ellery corrected, "I mean, yes. That sounds great!"

"Okay. Well." Jack was still brisk, still businesslike, but now Ellery was pretty sure that was just Jack feeling self-conscious. He knew because *he* felt self-conscious.

"I'll be in touch." Jack stepped back and nodded good night.

"Night," Ellery said.

"Good night." Jack added, in afterthought, "Maybe I should wait to see if your car starts."

Ellery chuckled, climbed into the VW, and the engine roared instantly to life just as though a flooded carburetor was something that only happened to other cars.

He raised his hand in farewell, pulling slowly, circumspectly past Jack, so as not to spray him with gravel.

He was smiling all the drive home—at least until he remembered he had left Watson with his puppy-sitter back in Pirate's Cove.

CHAPTER FOUR

"You're in a good mood this morning," Nora observed on Tuesday.

"Yes, I am." Ellery was making the most of no customers in the Crow's Nest to play his version of hide-and-seek with Watson.

Upon hearing his voice, Watson came charging out of the Romantic Suspense section to chase Ellery down to where he was crouching behind the circular sale rack.

"You found me!" Ellery exclaimed, and Watson jumped up and down with excitement and tried to bite his nose.

Watching them, Nora smiled faintly and shook her head.

Ellery *was* in a good mood. Sure, Brandon's presence in Pirate's Cove was a little bit of a raincloud, but otherwise, the outlook seemed pretty darned sunny this morning. Not that he wanted to make too much of a simple invitation to dinner. He was not looking for any complications in his life. But he did really enjoy spending time with Jack. He was open to—even eager to—see more of him.

"Janet Maples is out of the hospital. I saw her getting coffee at the Brewhouse."

"That's good news," Ellery said. And then, "Hey! No biting!"

Watson drew back as though to say, *Who me?* and then licked Ellery's face in apology.

"She said she heard from Ernest Burke that his company has been hired to do the renovations on Skull House. They're going to begin by knocking down half the walls on the ground level. Your friend wants an open floor plan." Nora said the words *open floor plan* like the design concept was an affront to humanity.

Yeah, no way that would go over well with Nora or any of the other members of the Pirate's Cove Historical Society.

Ellery sighed, got to his feet, and joined Nora behind the counter. "Brandon isn't my friend. We used to know each other a long time ago, and we didn't exactly part on good terms. But, Nora, you had to know he wasn't going to live in Skull House as is."

"He should respect the architectural integrity of the property. Regardless of who owns it, that building belongs to the entire island."

"Welllllll…" Ellery didn't want to argue with Nora while she was still so upset, and he too didn't like the idea of a historic building's integrity being compromised, but as much as he sympathized with her feelings, he couldn't agree with her reasoning.

He was pretty sure the law was *not* on Nora's side.

"Skull House should never have been sold to him," Nora was saying. "It's a...a travesty. I'm going to start a petition while there's still time to stop him from destroying everything."

Ellery considered and discarded a couple of comments. "When does demolition begin?"

"I can't get a straight answer. Within a day or so. He's talking about holding an auction this weekend to sell off the furniture and fixtures that still remain, according to Ernest."

According to Ernest, according to Janet, according to whoever. The island's internal communication system was efficient, if not always accurate.

"You have to do what you feel is right," Ellery said, "but don't get your hopes too high. Unless Brandon has changed a lot through the years, he isn't going to care what anyone on this island thinks or says or does."

Nora said grimly, "He may not have a choice."

Ohhhkay.

Ellery didn't bother to answer. Nora would just have to learn the same as everyone else who tried to get between Brandon and what he wanted. In any case, their monthly shipment of books had arrived, and Ellery got to work unpacking boxes and logging the titles into the computer system so that Nora could pull orders before he began shelving the fresh inventory.

Now and again, the bell on the door would chime and someone would drift into the bookshop, asking after Brandon's books. It was sort of funny but also sort of irritating—the Crow's Nest was a mystery bookstore, and Brandon's work fell mostly in the realm of spec fiction—and almost none of the requests came from regular customers. But maybe that was the wrong way to look at it. The goal of every business was to expand their customer base, and if the people of Pirate's Cove were eager to read Brandon's work, why not give them what they wanted? Brandon's books probably held enough elements of mystery and intrigue to warrant a place on the shelves.

A couple of people even asked when Brandon would be doing an author reading and signing at the Crow's Nest. The idea made Ellery groan inside, but he smiled politely, and had Nora sign them up for the bookshop newsletter.

He was just shelving the final book, Harlan Coben's *The Boy from the Woods*, when the bell on the front door chimed once again and Brandon sauntered in.

"Look at you," he greeted Ellery. "You almost look like you know what you're doing behind that counter!"

Nora made a huffy little sound and retreated to the back office without another word.

"Something I said?" Brandon asked.

"Isn't it usually?" Ellery replied.

Brandon smirked. "Usually," he agreed.

He wore his traditional black jeans and black turtleneck, but these days the turtleneck was cashmere and the jeans looked like snakeskin. He looked like a successful and wealthy eccentric, which was pretty much what he was.

"To what do I owe this honor?" Ellery asked.

"You're the only bookstore in town." Brandon cast his gaze over the seascapes hanging on the walls, the tall, neatly organized shelves, the row of gleaming ships' lanterns lining the back wall. "So this is it. This is your second act?"

"*Ta-da!*" Ellery retorted. "Yep."

Brandon's smile was rueful. "I hate to say it, but it kind of suits you."

"I know," Ellery admitted. "I kind of enjoy it."

Brandon glanced around. "No endcap of local authors?"

"If you're asking whether we carry your books, nope. We don't." Honesty compelled Ellery to add, "But it seems I'll be ordering some soon. People have been asking for them."

Brandon looked smug. "Naturally."

"Still as humble as ever."

"Why should I be? Four of my last five books have been *New York Times* bestsellers."

"Not your last one." As soon as the words were out, Ellery felt mean-spirited. He had checked, though, first thing that morning, and Brandon's last book had—all things being relative—tanked.

"The next one will be a doozy." He glanced past Ellery to the doorway Nora had disappeared through. "Water under the bridge. That's not why I'm here. Although, I've got a bunch of author copies on hand, if you want to sell them. You can have them for free. I don't do anything with them. They just take up space."

"Really?" That was unexpectedly generous, especially coming from Brandon.

"Sure. It's good promotion for me. Seeing this is going to be my home base." He grinned. "Well, not *this*. But Buck Island."

"Yeah, I'm still wondering about that," Ellery said. "You're the last person in the world I'd picture being happy living on a little island in the middle of nowhere."

"Why not? You're happy here. Anyway, you don't know me. You never really did, but you sure as heck don't know me now."

Ellery shrugged. "Fair enough."

"The real reason I'm here is to apologize for last night. I didn't realize Elliot Parker was such a deep dark secret."

"He—it—is not."

"It sure seemed like it. The way you recoiled, you'd think I pulled your pants down." Brandon waggled his eyebrows. "Which, as I recall—"

"Okay, stop." Ellery was not kidding.

Brandon made a face. "You didn't use to be such a prude."

"I'm not a prude. But we're not in college either." Ellery tried to find a diplomatic way to get his feelings across. "I'm a businessman. This is my community. That part of my life is over. Okay?"

"And you're embarrassed about it."

"Not really. I mean, they were terrible movies, and I was terrible in them, but they were fun at first, and I made money. I understand why you maybe feel a little defensive about the character of Noah Street, but you didn't actually write all those screenplays, so I'm not sure why you're taking any of this personally."

"I think you know why."

"I don't."

"Nobody is that clueless."

"I am." Ellery reconsidered. "Uh, that is, I have no idea what you're getting at."

"Come to dinner with me on Saturday, and I'll spell it out for you."

Ellery sighed. "I can't. It's opening night."

"For what?"

This was a little uncomfortable.

"I'm involved with the local theater group."

Brandon looked horrified. "You're acting in *community* theater?"

"Not exactly. The point is, I've got plans."

"Okay. Tonight."

"Rehearsal."

Brandon got that stubborn look Ellery remembered only too well. "Tomorrow night."

"I've got a date." Ellery couldn't help smiling at the thought of Jack.

Brandon frowned. "With who?"

"What does it matter?"

"Thursday, then?"

"Rehearsal."

Brandon said slowly, "I don't believe it. You're *afraid* to go out with me."

Ellery laughed with real amusement. "Nope. Not at all. I just have other things going on. We could meet for drinks on Friday after dress rehearsal, if you'd like. There's a wine bar on Church Street that will stay open until eleven if they've got customers."

Brandon considered, then shrugged. "I guess I'll have to take what I can get. Seeing that you're in such demand."

Ellery made a face. He knew sarcasm when he heard it.

"What's the name of the wine bar?"

"Wine and Rosés."

"Cute."

"It's a cute little village."

"Maybe on the surface," Brandon said. He didn't seem to be kidding. At Ellery's look of surprise, he said, "Are you saying you don't know about the Witherspoon case?"

"The Witherspoon case? Never heard of it."

Brandon glanced past Ellery again toward the office door. "Your cute little village has a murky history."

Ellery snorted.

"I'm not kidding."

"Sure you are."

"There are dark undercurrents here. I'll fill you in on Friday."

The air of mystery, i.e., manufactured drama, was like the Brandon of old. "Sure," Ellery said, unimpressed. "See you then."

Brandon didn't hang around long after that. When the bell above the door signaled his departure, Nora reemerged, conveniently done with whatever she'd been pretending to do for the last ten minutes.

"I don't think we need to get carried away stocking his books," she announced. "People are curious about him, that's all. They'll have their fill soon enough. His last book was a flop. I looked it up."

"Yeah, but the others have done well. He's not a bad writer." Ellery was grudging but honest.

Nora eyed him, as though trying to make up her mind about something. She said finally, "You should be careful of him, dearie. I know his type. He likes mixing things up, stirring the pot."

"*Is* there something to stir up?" Ellery asked, watching her.

Nora was no longer looking at him. She tidied the desk counter, repositioned the small bronze crow paperweight just so.

"Every town has its secrets," she said.

CHAPTER FIVE

Why the heck was he so *nervous*?

It was just a meal between friends.

Well, no. Jack had specifically said it was a date.

Which was great. Right? Given how attracted he was to Jack? Except…maybe he was *too* attracted to Jack. Ellery was in a good place right now; mostly over the hurt inflicted by Todd's betrayal, and content with his own company. He had plenty to keep him busy. He was, well, happy. Granted, he'd be happier if the bookshop was doing well, happier if the roof at Captain's Seat didn't leak and the chimney didn't smoke, but still. Life was good.

He finished shaving for the second time that day and scowled at his reflection in the silvered mirror over the sink in the tiny back bathroom at the Crow's Nest. *Don't make too much of this.*

A dab of hair gel wouldn't hurt. The sea air tended to turn his wavy dark brown hair curly, and because he hadn't bothered with a haircut in weeks, he looked a little…crazed. Not as crazed as he had before he trimmed his eyebrows with his desk scissors. Ellery studied his reflection ruefully. Hopefully it was the dingy lighting giving his hazel eyes that hollow, haunted look. It could be worse. He had good bones, good skin, and perfect—thank you, Mom and Dad, for the braces—teeth. Which was lucky because these days his entire grooming arsenal consisted of aftershave and lip balm. Hey, his jeans were clean and his black lambswool sweater smelled only faintly of mothballs. What more could a guy ask for?

It's not like Pirate's Cove was teaming with members of the LGBTQ community. As far as Ellery could tell, he and Jack seemed to be it, and Jack was bisexual.

At least, that was Ellery's assumption. They hadn't ever really discussed it. And that would be because they hadn't really discussed a lot of things. In fact, as Ellery thought about it, he had to admit he really didn't know a whole heck of a lot about Jack. They talked plenty, sure, but it was never about anything serious. Never anything really personal. He talked about the book business, and Jack talked about police work. They shared amusing anecdotes about their day—one of the things Ellery did for sure like about Jack was the fact that they had similar senses of humor. And they shared that fish-out-of-water worldview of Pirate's Cove.

Oh, and they talked quite a bit about home renovation. Jack turned out to know *a lot* about things like knob and tube wiring and thinset mortar—in fact, *that* was something Jack had shared: his father had owned his own construction company. Jack had been appalled the first time he'd seen Ellery trying to rip up old linoleum without safety glasses or a reusable respirator.

If Ellery was being completely honest, part of what he enjoyed about Jack was the lack of any kind of emotional demand. He found Jack handsome, for sure he liked spending time with him, but he was uneasy about moving their friendship to the next level.

He did not have good luck with relationships, and was afraid to jeopardize his friendship with Jack.

"So then don't," he told his reflection.

His date prep complete, Ellery checked the time. Nearly six. He was aggravated at the butterflies swarming through his stomach. Or maybe it was the pastrami he had for lunch. He grabbed his jacket, bundled up Watson and took him next door to deliver him to Sandy's daughter's care, and by the time he arrived back at the Crow's Nest, Jack was standing outside the locked front door, peering through it.

Jack had changed from his uniform to jeans and what looked like a white Aran sweater beneath his sheepskin jacket. His hair looked damp, and Ellery caught a whiff of herbal aftershave.

He glanced around at the sound of Ellery's approaching footsteps, and smiled, his teeth very white in the gloom.

"I thought you forgot."

Ellery smiled back, his heart lightening, his earlier angst forgotten. "No, just leaving Watson with his babysitter."

They grinned at each other, maybe a little self-consciously, and Jack said, "Do you need anything from inside?"

"No. I'm ready. Where are we going?" He fell into step beside Jack as they headed down the street toward the harbor.

"I was thinking maybe we'd take the ferry to Point Judith."

"Really?"

Jack nodded. "It's about thirty minutes each way, but there's more variety of places to eat."

"Sure," Ellery said. More variety and more privacy. He got it. He was pretty sure most of Pirate's Cove believed their police chief to be one hundred percent heterosexual. He had no intention of dating anyone in the closet, but so far this was just dinner out. No need to strike a pose.

As though reading his mind, Jack said, "People like to talk, and that's fine. I'm used to it, but you're still an unknown quantity for a lot of folks. I don't want..." He hesitated.

"I think most people have figured out I'm gay."

"Oh, yeah." Jack agreed so readily, it startled Ellery. "That's not what I mean."

"Then what *do* you mean?"

"I think part of the problem with what happened with Sue was everyone was speculating about us, about whether we were a couple or not, and it created pressure. I'm not even sure why. I liked Sue, but there weren't any romantic feelings on my part."

So, did that mean... What *did* that mean? That Jack had no romantic feelings for Ellery and didn't want people to think he did?

"Sure." Even Ellery could hear how doubtful he sounded.

Jack seemed to choose his words. "I think it would be nice to see where this goes, but I don't want to turn you into the topic du jour. More than you already are. Does that make sense?"

Actually, it did. And actually, Ellery appreciated both the honesty and what was, at least partly, a chivalrous gesture.

"Yes. It makes sense. And...I'd like to see where this goes too."

Once again, they gazed into each other's eyes and smiled.

* * * * *

They dined fireside on the patio at Spain of Narragansett, a large and casually elegant restaurant that specialized in Spanish and Mediterranean seafood.

The meal started with Clams Casino and a couple of glasses of white wine, and Ellery decided Jack had been right to get them off Buck Island for the evening. This was the most relaxed Ellery had ever seen him.

"I don't think I told you how nice you look to-night," Jack said after they toasted to "Happy memories."

Ellery grinned. His black jeans and sweater were a far cry from the faded Levi's and chunky sweaters he typically wore. "It's my eyebrows. I trimmed them, so I look less crazy."

Jack chuckled. "That was one of the things that surprised me about you. You don't look like someone with a sense of humor."

Ellery snorted. He knew what Jack meant, though. More than once he had been described in a review as "broodingly handsome," which, given how totally UNbroody he was, was especially embarrassing. "Laughter is the best medicine. I really believe that."

Jack's mouth twisted. He nodded. "Laughter and Scotch."

"I've never seen you drink Scotch."

"I don't. Not anymore."

Hmm... There was backstory there for sure, but the suddenly bleak look in Jack's gaze warned Ellery this was not the moment to probe.

Their meals arrived then. Shrimp and saffron paella for Ellery. Rack of lamb for Jack. Jack, who turned out to know his way around a wine menu, ordered another bottle, this time a rich Viognier.

It had been months since Ellery had enjoyed this kind of leisurely, luxurious meal with a friend. The food was great. The service was great. He was enjoying himself even more than he'd hoped.

"How long would you say it took before you stopped feeling like an outsider?" he asked Jack.

"In Pirate's Cove?" Jack considered. "About a year, I guess." He added, "But as far as the village is concerned, we're always going to be outsiders."

"You think so?"

"Yep. I do. If you weren't born on the island, you're an outsider. That's not to say you won't be welcome. You *are* welcome." Jack added ruefully, "More so than me."

"*I* am?" Ellery was skeptical.

"Definitely. Partly, that's because your family roots stretch all the way to the island's bedrock. Partly, well, you fit in here."

Ellery laughed.

"Yeah, but I'm not kidding," Jack said. "You're restoring Captain's Seat to its former glory. That makes a lot of people happy. You joined the theater group, you joined the Monday Night Scrabblers, and you've done a good job turning the bookshop into a much-needed social center."

"That last is mostly Nora's doing," Ellery admitted.

Jack shrugged. "Regardless of whose idea it was, the Crow's Nest—*you*—are weaving yourself into the community fabric."

Ellery thought that over. He sort of liked the idea, although he wasn't sure Jack was correct. After another swallow of wine, he asked, "Would you say Pirate's Cove has, er, dark undercurrents?"

Jack's eyebrows shot up. "Dark undercurrents? I take it this is not an oceanography question?"

"Not an oceanography question."

"Okay, well, I'm not exactly sure what you mean."

Neither was Ellery. "It's hard to put into words. Sometimes I do kind of feel like everyone in the village except me is in on a secret."

Jack said wryly, "That's a full-time feeling when you're a cop."

"Is it? Hm. I bet it is."

Jack studied him. "Anything in particular spark this sense of unease?"

Sense of unease was a good way to put it. Except, Ellery hadn't had a sense of unease until Brandon began uttering cryptic comments. And his disquiet was more to do with Brandon than any village undercurrent.

"Something Brandon said."

Jack made a noncommittal noise.

The conversation turned then to different channels.

"Do you dive, by any chance?" Jack asked after they had covered local politics, the play rehearsals, and Janet Maples' safe return to village life.

"You mean like scuba diving?"

Jack nodded. "There are a lot of great diving sites off the island. A lot of shipwrecks to explore."

"Shipwrecks? As in sunken treasure?"

Jack's cheek creased. "Depending on your definition of treasure."

"I don't dive, but I'm a strong swimmer. I'm sure I could learn."

Jack's smile made Ellery feel warm inside. "I'm sure I could teach you."

So *that* was promising.

As they neared the end of their meal, Jack asked very casually, "What's the story on your friend Brandon?"

"What do you mean?" Hadn't they already covered this?

Jack's bright gaze seemed suddenly intent. "He was down at the station today, asking to see some cold-case files."

Ellery blinked. "Cold-case files?"

"That's right. Has he talked to you about what he's working on?"

"No. Why? What's he working on?"

Instead of answering, Jack said, "I can't quite figure him out. Is he as oblivious as he seems?"

"I'm still not sure what you're talking about." But the answer to that question was yes. Definitely.

"Do you think he would confide in you?"

"About what?" Ellery was starting to feel uneasy. "He stopped by the Crow's Nest yesterday, but I think that was to ask me out."

This time Jack's eyebrows nearly hit his hairline. "To ask you out?"

"People do."

Jack made a sound of not-quite-humor. "I know they do. I thought you two weren't on cozy terms."

"*Cozy?*" Ellery repeated. "That's an interesting word choice. No, we're not on cozy terms, but if he's going to be living on the island, I figure I need to try to get along with him."

"That's probably wise."

Ellery shrugged. He viewed it more as self-preservation.

Jack studied him. "You think he wants to get back together with you?"

Ellery almost spit his wine out. He gulped it down, said, "Get back together? No way."

"He seemed pretty...focused on you Monday night."

"I don't know what that was about other than making me uncomfortable—which he would enjoy because he likes making everybody uncomfortable. But no. First of all, we were both sick of each other by the time we split up, and secondly, it was never any great love affair to start with. We were off and on in college, and then we moved in together because..."

"Because?"

"It seemed like a good idea at the time?" In hind-sight, it wasn't so much that they had made a decision as they had simply drifted into what had seemed con-venient and expedient.

"Friends with benefits?"

It was tempting to agree, but Ellery resisted the easy lie. "At first, yes. But then... No. We did—I did—try to have a real relationship, but—" He shook his head. "He wasn't relationship material. Not like Todd. That is, not in the same way Todd wasn't rela-tionship material. I don't think Brandon cheated on me. He was just so hard to get along with. Talented, for sure. But also moody and...difficult."

He didn't want to go into all that ancient history, but he should have known Jack wouldn't let it go. In-terrogation was probably programmed into his DNA.

"Difficult how?"

Ellery wanted to ask how this was relevant, but clearly, for Jack, it was relevant.

"It sounds so petty now."

"You're not a petty person," Jack said. It wasn't so much a compliment as an observation.

"Trivial, then. A lot of little things that built into something that felt insurmountable. If that makes sense."

"Makes sense to me. For example?"

Ellery sighed. "He used to steal money from me. Not a lot, but pretty regularly."

Jack looked grim. "I don't think theft is trivial. Or petty."

"It was more pilfering than theft." Jack opened his mouth, and Ellery tried to head him off. "I know what you're going to say, but I don't want to exaggerate what happened. It was more irritating than anything. But I was already the one paying for almost everything. From our rent to drinks out. It was usually on me. To be fair, I was earning a lot more modeling back then, but Brandon also resented having to do his share of, well, really anything. Like household chores. He just wouldn't do them. Ever. Which sounds ridiculous, I know. But I mean, I don't think he washed a single cup or took out a single bag of trash in the six months we lived together."

Jack heard him out. He said, "My question is why you kept living with him for six months."

Ellery shook his head. "I'm not sure. I wouldn't put up with it now. But back then… You know how it is when you're young. At first, I thought he'd change. And then later, I kept waiting for the right time to break it off."

Jack's mouth curved ruefully. "'How it is when you're young'? You're still pretty young."

"You're not so much older."

"I am in cop years."

Ellery snorted, but maybe there was some truth in that. Despite their closeness in age, Jack did seem quite a bit older, quite a bit…harder sometimes.

"Anyway," Ellery said. He knew Jack was right. He wasn't even sure why he had let things drag on for so long. It hadn't been love, because he hadn't ever really been in love with Brandon. He *had* felt a little sorry for him, off and on, but mostly he had dreaded Brandon's reaction—and it had not been pleasant. True enough.

He admitted, "That wasn't even the worst of it. Brandon badmouthed me to our friends. And about such crazy things. That I was doing drugs, or that I was drunk all the time, or that I was stealing from *him*... It's not even like anyone believed him. It was just weird."

"Jesus," Jack said. "None of that is petty. I can't understand how you put up with it for six months."

"I don't either, really." Because the sex had been great? The sex *had* been great. "My point is, I don't have feelings for him anymore, and I don't think he ever *did* have feelings for me."

Wasn't it in the dating handbook not to talk about exes on the first date? The confusing part was Ellery didn't get the feeling that Jack was jealous or asking for personal reasons. In fact, Jack seemed to be strongly channeling Police Chief Carson.

"What's this all about? Why are you so interested in Brandon?"

Jack hesitated, and the unpleasant thought occurred to Ellery that maybe the real reason Jack had asked him out was to pump him for information on Brandon. But why?

Jack drained the rest of his wine and placed his glass on the table. "Has Brandon mentioned the name Rebecca Witherspoon to you?"

"Who?" But then memory clicked into place. "Wait. Yes. He did, in passing, mention the Witherspoon case."

"Did he tell you—"

"When I say 'in passing,' I mean literally in passing. He said Pirate's Cove had dark undercurrents, and he would tell me about the Witherspoon case when we have drinks."

Jack's brows drew together. "When you have drinks?"

This was awkward. Having spent five minutes bashing Brandon, he was now going to have to admit to planning to have drinks with him.

"Friday night. I agreed to meet him after dress rehearsal."

Jack's expression was Does Not Compute, and no wonder.

"I know," Ellery said, "but it seemed easier to meet him and hear what he has to say. Otherwise, it's liable to seem like a bigger deal than it is."

Jack said, "It's hard to follow your logic." Which was honest, if not tactful.

"I don't like to argue." Ellery meant he hadn't wanted to argue with Brandon, but maybe Jack thought he meant he didn't want to argue with *him* because his blue-green eyes narrowed.

"All right."

"No. I mean, I don't mind arguing with *you*—"

Jack gave a short laugh. "I've noticed."

Okay, possibly this was one of those situations where the more you tried to explain, the worse it got. Ellery said instead, "Anyway, who's Rebecca Witherspoon?"

Jack seemed only too happy to follow this redirect. "A local girl who disappeared twenty years ago."

"Disappeared? As in *vanished*?"

"As in made her escape after allegedly committing homicide."

"*Homicide?*" Ellery stared at him. In the firelight, Jack's face looked dark and unreadable. "You weren't kidding about a cold case. And this has something to do with Skull House? What happened?"

"It's everything to do with Skull House, given that the new owner is Brandon Abbott."

Right. Because Brandon wrote fictionalized accounts of real crimes.

"Okay, well, I hadn't heard anything about Rebecca Witherspoon and Skull House until now."

"No. Well, twenty years later, it's still a sensitive subject on the island."

Ellery was silent, waiting, and Jack said slowly, "Thirty years ago, Skull House was still being used as the summer home of the Tideworths. But eventually the family died off. The only one left was a maiden aunt in Boston."

"Do people still say maiden aunt?" Ellery asked.

Jack sighed.

"Sorry. Go on."

"Legally, the house wasn't abandoned, but since no one ever stayed there, the servants were all let go. There was a caretaker, but once he died, his position was never filled."

"The house just sat there?"

"Exactly. Fully furnished but uninhabited."

"Hm."

"Which naturally made it a tempting target for local teens."

"*Ah*. Right."

"As you'd expect, there were a few thefts, some vandalization, but basically, this is a pretty law-abiding island. For the most part the house just sat there collecting dust."

"Why wasn't it sold?"

Jack shook his head. "No idea. Obviously, this was way before my time. Anyway, one spring break, a group of kids came home from college, and a party was planned at Skull House—"

"I may have starred in this movie," Ellery said, and Jack gave him a crooked grin.

"I hope it ended better for Noah Street."

Was it goofy to be flattered that Jack remembered his character's name? Probably.

"What went wrong?"

"Nobody knows for sure. Or at least, no one has ever talked. The evening ended with one kid dead and another presumably on the run. Although she may well be dead too by now."

"*She* being Rebecca Witherspoon?"

"Correct."

"Who did she kill?"

"A kid named Steve Robertson. He had been a big football star in high school, but unlike Rebecca, he didn't go off to college. He stayed on the island and worked in the family business."

This really was beginning to sound like one of the *Happy Halloween* flicks. "Were they a couple?"

"No. No, but there was history there. Her friends later claimed the Robertson kid had been harassing her. His friends claimed she was a tease, that she had been coming on to him. We may never know. Like I said, no one ever talked. We don't have rumors so much as rumors of rumors."

"In all this time? On an island this small?" In Ellery's experience, gossip was a major pastime in Pirate's Cove. It was hard to believe the truth hadn't come out in twenty long years.

Jack shrugged. "I tried to reopen the case when I first moved here. I didn't get any further than my predecessors. This is one secret the people of Pirate's Cove keep to themselves."

"But why, though? Why wouldn't the islanders want this solved?"

"I honestly don't know. I thought the same thing in the beginning. Maybe there's a feeling of shared guilt? Shared responsibility for what happened—or what didn't happen in the way of adult supervision? Two years ago, one of those true-crime shows tried to get permission to do an episode on Skull House. They offered a lot of money, but the town fathers shot it down. Not that I blame them. I didn't want a film crew here either. I figured they'd destroy whatever might be left of the crime scene. It's moot now."

Yes. Because Brandon owned the property. Brandon had already hired contractors to start ripping the house apart.

Ellery said, "Brandon uses real crimes as the basis of his stories, but he doesn't do any serious investigation. In his books, the true culprit is always supernatural. Like a demon or a ghost or a vampire."

"That may be, but I'm still getting complaints."

"From who?"

"Hard to say. They're being funneled through the mayor's office. Suffice it to say, Abbott's stirring up bad memories."

Ellery thought that over. "How did she—Rebecca—kill Steve?"

"He was bludgeoned to death with a marble bust. Supposedly, a replica of John Mansfield."

"Supposedly? If the case remains unsolved, wouldn't the murder weapon still be held in an evidence locker?" That was how it worked in most mystery novels.

"Somewhere along the line, it disappeared, along with any other physical evidence there may have been."

"That seems...pretty strange."

"I'll say." Jack's tone was grim.

"And there was never any trace of Rebecca? She'd have had to leave the island on the ferry, wouldn't she?"

"Spring break twenty years ago? It's possible she could have managed to slip away. Robertson's body wasn't discovered for two days. Or she could have sailed to the mainland. She was supposed to be an accomplished sailor."

Ellery had not been working in a mystery bookshop for four months for nothing. "A boat would have been missing, though, right?"

"Right. But the fact that it wasn't reported doesn't mean it didn't happen. Someone may have covered for her."

"I see your point." Ellery considered. "Why does everyone assume Rebecca killed Steve? Especially since no one knows who else was at the party?"

Jack made a face. "Aside from the fact that they had history, it seems that Witherspoon was a descendant of Ann Rathbone."

"So what?" Light dawned. "Oh. I get it. History repeats itself? Steve attacked her, she defended herself, and then...what? Jumped into the ocean?"

"It's one theory." Jack's tone was neutral. "The Witherspoon girl killed herself after she conked the Robertson kid on the head."

"Is that what you think happened?"

"I have some problems with the...synchronicity of that. The girl just happens to be related to Rathbone. She just happens to grab a bust of Mansfield.

She just happens to vanish beneath the waves. It seems pretty unlikely."

"A little too on the nose," agreed Ellery the screenwriter. "But the Robertson kid was killed and Rebecca did disappear. That's for sure?"

"Those two facts remain."

"Wow," Ellery murmured. "Is it possible Rebecca didn't kill Robertson, but saw who did and ran away because she was afraid of that person?"

"It's possible. It's even possible Rebecca eventually returned to the island and lives here now under a different name."

"Are you—" Ellery caught the glint in Jack's eye, and subsided. He made a face. "Sure it is."

Jack's grin held friendly mockery. "Or not." He wasn't teasing, however, when he added, "It's a mystery, and people love mysteries, but when you have drinks with your ex, you might remind him that sometimes it's smarter to let sleeping dogs lie."

"Smarter?" Ellery asked slowly. "Or safer?"

Jack didn't hesitate. "Both."

CHAPTER SIX

It wasn't that Ellery thought he and Jack were now going steady.

It wasn't that he expected their relationship to change drastically—or maybe even at all.

When Jack didn't drop by the Crow's Nest on Thursday morning, Ellery tried not to make too much of it. Even when Jack didn't stop by on Friday, he tried not to see it as significant. After all, Jack didn't stop by every single morning. Well, actually, for the last month, he *had* stopped by pretty much every single morning. It wasn't like they had a plan or an arrangement. Sometimes Jack brought Ellery coffee, sometimes Ellery picked up coffee for Jack, sometimes they made lunch plans, sometimes they didn't do more than wish each other a good day.

That casual morning ritual was something Ellery looked forward to, so he probably would have noticed Jack's absence either way, but he wouldn't have instantly assumed the worst.

Okay, *the worst* was a bit dramatic, but something had gone wrong.

He didn't *want* to think it, because he had enjoyed having dinner with Jack. Overall, he felt their date had gone well. Jack had not kissed him good night, not even a peck on the cheek, but it hadn't quite felt like the right moment, so it hadn't bothered Ellery. Not *that* much. Not then.

Looking back now on Wednesday night, he had to wonder.

It did seem like toward the end of dinner, Jack's mood had changed, grown less flirtatious and date-like and more...Everybody's Favorite Police Chief Carson. He had still been friendly and attentive, but yeah, there had been a shift in attitude.

Try as he might, Ellery couldn't quite pinpoint when the change had taken place. Was it when Jack had learned Ellery was going to have drinks with Brandon, or had it been earlier? Or later? Had he spent too much time bashing Brandon? Probably.

Or was he imagining the change in mood?

When they'd parted ways, Jack had not said anything about getting together again. Not for a date, not for anything. But since they saw each other every day, why would he?

He didn't want to overthink it. He and Jack were bound to see plenty of each other, whether they went out again or not. The evening had ended on a friendly note, so why make too much of it? Any of it?

He was determined not to.

"Well? How did it go, dearie?" Nora asked when she arrived at the Crow's Nest that morning. Nora had Thursdays off, so Ellery had not spoken to her for a day.

Ellery stared, asked uneasily, "How did what go?"

"Dinner with Police Chief Carson, of course."

"How do you know about that?"

Nora looked amused. "It's hard to imagine what else the two of you would be doing catching the 6:10 ferry Wednesday night."

"You saw us?"

"Mrs. Nelson saw you. And Mr. Starling. And Mrs. Smith."

"How the— Were they lurking outside the building?"

Nora laughed, but her expression changed, hardened as the bell on the door swayed in lazy welcome and Brandon strolled in.

As Nora disappeared into the back office, Brandon laughed. "The old lady does *not* like me," he said. "If I wind up dead, there's the number-one suspect."

Ellery retorted, "Don't be so sure."

Brandon beamed. "You could be more right than you know. We still on for tonight?"

Ellery sighed. "I guess."

Brandon's face tightened. "Don't sound so enthusiastic."

"Hey. Getting together was your idea. I've got a lot going on. Rehearsal could run late tonight. I'm not sure why this can't wait."

"You're seriously putting an amateur-hour rehearsal over meeting with me?"

Hell to the yes. But Ellery tried to be diplomatic. "I committed to being there."

"You committed to me too."

"I shouldn't have. What's the big deal with having drinks together? You haven't been interested in seeing me in how many years? What's the urgency?"

Brandon threw a strange look at the open door to the back office. "I'll tell you tonight."

"*Brandon.*"

"All right, all right." Brandon lowered his voice. "I need your help."

"With *what*?"

Brandon said so quietly, Ellery had to lean forward to hear properly, "I need your detective skills."

"My— *Huh*?"

"Your detective skills."

"You're kidding."

"No, I'm not kidding. You solved that murder you were accused of, didn't you?"

"I didn't solve it. I fell over the solution when I was playing Scrabble. It's not the same thing."

Over in the Cozy Mystery section, Mrs. Smith cleared her throat.

Brandon threw a quick look over his shoulder. "*Shhhh!*"

"*You* shush," Ellery retorted irritably. Actually, he had forgotten Mrs. Smith was still in the store. It was easy to overlook her.

"Look, I don't want to talk about it here. You promised to meet me. I'm holding you to that promise."

"You're *holding* me to it?"

"I am."

"You can't— You're unreal, Brandon. You know that?"

"Of course." Brandon spared him a superior smile. "It's why I'm more interesting than other people."

He wasn't joking either. Brandon believed it. Ellery gave a disbelieving laugh. But as tempting as it was to tell Brandon to take a long walk off a short pier, he was—unwillingly—curious what all this was about. "*Fine.* I'll see you tonight, unless I get held up."

"Just be there," Brandon told him.

"Or what?"

"Or you'll be sorry."

"It won't be the first time."

"And it won't be the last time." Brandon knew better than to waste a good exit line. He pointed at Ellery, turned, and strode from the bookshop, letting the front door slam shut behind him with a sharp jangle of bells.

"What an unpleasant man," Mrs. Smith said, suddenly appearing at the counter. "What was he threatening you about?"

Nora stepped from the office. "Is he gone?"

"Yes, he's gone," Ellery said.

Nora scowled at the bell still swinging against the door. "It's a shame," she muttered, "just a shame he doesn't disappear like..." She trailed off when she realized Ellery and Mrs. Smith were staring at her.

* * * * *

"Bravo!" Dylan clapped approval as dress rehearsal wound up. "BRA-VO!"

The house lights came up. Dylan's slightly self-conscious, slightly smug cast, clad in their 1920s costumes, practiced their final bows, and then everyone scrambled off the stage to gather around the director and Ellery.

"Wow. Great job!" Ellery said.

"Surprised?" Libby teased, fluttering her false eyelashes.

"Well, yeah," he admitted, and everyone laughed.

Ellery *was* pleasantly surprised at how well this final rehearsal had gone. He knew the Scallywags were an enthusiastic bunch, but he had taken it for granted their performance would be less than impressive. And the weeks of slightly chaotic rehearsal that had gone before seemed to validate his doubt. He'd been wrong. Everything went exactly the way it was supposed to. No one forgot their lines. No one missed their cue. Lights and sound were perfect. He'd been involved in messier professional productions for sure.

"We have a wonderful script, after all," Dylan said, more loyally than accurately, in Ellery's opinion, but he grinned good-naturedly at the compliment.

Felix said, "Yeah, yeah. We're going to kill it tomorrow! Now let's get dressed and go get wasted!"

"*Uhhhhhhhh*," Dylan began, and there was more laughter. Neither Felix nor Libby were twenty-one, but it didn't seem to be much of an issue. Libby even worked for her father in the Salty Dog most evenings. You'd think Mr. Law and Order Chief Carson would have something to say about that, but apparently not.

Less than forty minutes later, the Scallywags filled the long tables that had been shoved together in the center of the Salty Dog, and Tom Tulley was circulating with trays of drinks while cast and crew babbled excitedly about Saturday's sold out opening night.

Ellery couldn't help looking for Jack, but there was no sign of him in the pub that evening. No sign of Brandon either, but he hadn't expected to see Brandon.

Not until later, anyway. Unless he could think of a decent excuse to duck out of drinks at Wine and Rosés.

"Well, my boy, do you feel we're doing you justice?" Mayor Cyrus Jones squeezed into the chair next to Ellery's.

Ellery blinked, shook off his preoccupation. "Oh, the play. Yes, I do. I'm very happy with how it's going."

Cyrus beamed. He was about fifty, a little portly, a little gray. The kind of person who seemed to be born middle-aged. The mayor's chubby and clean-shaven face gave him a naive look, but he was a shrewd businessman and a tenacious politician, having recently been reelected to a second five-year term of office.

"I bet you're a little surprised too."

"I am, true."

The mayor leaned forward, saying earnestly, "Can I ask you something?"

"Sure," Ellery said uneasily, as everyone is when asked that particular question in that particular tone.

"You made your living on the big screen. What do you think of Felix's talent? Do you think he has a future?"

"As an actor?"

Cyrus nodded. His brown eyes were solemn. It was no secret that Felix, Cyrus's only child by his second wife, Philippa, was the apple of his father's eye.

"I think he's genuinely talented," Ellery said. "But acting is a really tough business. It's not just about talent."

"I know." Cyrus sighed. "But his heart is set on a movie career."

Ellery, having no experience of parenting, said, "Well, I guess if you want to be supportive, you have to let him take his best shot."

"What do you think about the New York Acting School for Film and Television?"

"From what I hear, it's a great school. I don't have any personal experience with it."

That didn't seem to matter to the mayor. He rambled on about Felix's hopes and dreams for a life on the silver screen, and Ellery nodded politely, commented vaguely, and tried to flag Tom Tulley down for another drink.

When at last Cyrus turned his attention elsewhere, Ellery surreptitiously checked his phone and saw he had a voice message.

His heart rose. Jack? He immediately squelched the thought. Of course it wouldn't be Jack. No, more likely this was Brandon. Maybe cancelling? His heart rose again.

He pressed Playback and put the phone to his ear, frowning at the garbled rush of sound.

What the…

Sorry, wrong number?

He played the message again, and thought he recognized Brandon's voice. Was he speaking from a wind tunnel?

Ellery pushed his chair back, rose from the table, and stepped outside to listen again.

The night air was refreshingly cool after the crowded warmth of the pub. Behind the bright windows, he could hear voices and laughter and music.

Even in the quiet of the empty street, Ellery could only make out a couple of words in the garbled message: *house* and *help*. Which could have meant anything. Brandon could have been postponing. Brandon could have been trying to coerce him into driving out to Skull House.

What raised the hair on his scalp was Brandon's voice, the note of panic that filtered through the blast of static.

Even so. Not his problem, right?

So why was he hitting Call Back?

He was, though. Ellery pressed the button and waited. And waited. And waited.

Brandon's voice-mail message came on. The prerecorded Brandon sounded aggravatingly cocky. "Hey. Brandon here. You know what to do."

"Yes, I do," Ellery muttered, clicking off.

Yet here he was walking back inside the pub, pulling out his wallet, paying his bill, shrugging off Dylan's questions of why he was leaving and where he was going.

Ellery shook his head. "Brandon left me a weird message."

"He's a weird guy," Dylan said.

"I know. We were supposed to meet for drinks, though."

"Oh-*ho*!" Dylan winked broadly.

"No way," Ellery said, tucking his wallet back in his jeans. Sue Lewis, the mayor, and a handful of others watched him with open curiosity.

Dylan said, "No? Then why are you meeting him?"

Ellery muttered, "Good question." He raised his hand in farewell, but by then most of the group had returned to their drinks and talk.

* * * * *

Of course, first he had to jog back to Sandy's to retrieve Watson and then his car from the alley behind the Crow's Nest. On his way out of the village he stopped at Wine and Rosés just to make sure Brandon wasn't waiting for him.

The lights were muted. A sign hung in the front door. The wine bar was already closed for the evening. So much for that idea. Had Brandon stopped by, seen the bar was closed, and placed an irate phone call? Or was he actually in some kind of trouble?

Torn between apprehension and the suspicion he was being punked—this mysterious phone call business would be right up Brandon's alley—Ellery jumped back in his VW and sped out of town, heading toward Skull House on the northwestern tip of the island.

It was about a half hour drive in the opposite direction of Captain's Seat. The road was unpaved and unlit. Occasionally, he passed an abandoned barn or a couple of sleeping cows, but there were no other cars to be seen in either direction. Long stretches of highway were nearly engulfed by black swallowwort and Japanese knotweed as the ribbon of moonlit road wound through uninhabited hills and dunes.

At last, Pequot Bluffs and the house came into view.

Ellery's foot eased on the gas. He had only ever seen Skull House in the daylight, and that had been enough. By moonlight it looked like something off a gothic romance cover. One of those 1970s Lancer Easy Eye romantic suspensers with a stylishly clad girl fleeing from a ginormous architectural monstrosity of a house with a single light burning in a single window. Very energy efficient those gothic housekeepers.

In this case, there was no fleeing damsel in distress, and no lights shone from any window, but otherwise…yeah, pretty much.

He pressed the gas, approaching the house at a more sedate—and doubtful—pace, eventually pulling up in the overgrown drive.

For a moment, Ellery sat unmoving, the VW's engine idling. He watched the enormous silver moon drift in and out of cloud cover, and his unease grew.

Not that he had any specific concerns. Mostly he didn't trust Brandon.

It would be so like Brandon to drag him out to the back end of the island on some made-up excuse—or for the childish pleasure of jumping out from behind a giant urn to shout BOO! And yet… He glanced at Watson sleeping peacefully on the back seat. It was just possible something bad really had happened, something like a fall down stairs or—given the state of the house—a fall through the floor. Brandon could be lying in the cellar with a broken leg right now.

"Why is it *my* problem?" Ellery complained.

Watson raised his head, blinked sleepily, and tucked himself into a tighter ball.

Ellery sighed, climbed out of the car, pulling his collar up against the wind gusting up from the ocean beneath the bluff. He could hear—feel—the pound of the surf beneath his feet. Year by year, the ocean had gnawed at earth until there were only a few yards stretching between the edge and the house itself. One of these days the ocean would swallow Skull House and all its secrets. But that was surely still decades away.

Ellery turned and hiked up the broken walkway, stopping short when he was close enough to see the front door.

It stood wide open.

Or was that a trick of moonlight?

He approached slowly, cautiously, and saw that it was not a trick of the light. The front door *was* open.

Not good.

Never was a front door standing ajar in the middle of the night going to be a good thing.

Ellery sucked in a sharp breath, took another unwilling step forward, peering into the darkness beyond the reach of moonlight. He could smell varnish, sawdust and, unexpectedly, bacon.

"Brandon?" He peered through the dark oblong of doorway. "Are you in here?"

No answer.

Ellery took another reluctant step forward. He could see the checkerboard of floor and the ghostly outline of dustsheets. Nothing moved. There was no sound except his own quickened breathing.

Scratch that last. Back in the VW, Watson began to bark, his shrill protests at finding himself alone bouncing off the blank stony facade of the house.

ARF. ARF. ARF.

Talk about a voice to wake the dead.

"Brandon?" Ellery called again, more strongly. "Anyone home?"

The dark beyond the entryway seemed to swallow his voice.

The hair rose on the back of his neck. His heart began to thump in his ears.

He took a step back, then another, retreating from that tomblike silence.

As owner and proprietor of a mystery bookshop, Ellery was well aware that standard protocol demanded he squelch his trepidation, ignore his instincts, and enter the house to search for Brandon.

Instead, he withdrew another step, felt for his cell, and phoned Jack.

CHAPTER SEVEN

Jack picked up on the second ring. "What's up?" His tone was brisk.

Ellery didn't fail to notice the lack of warmth in Jack's voice, but he had bigger and more pressing problems than whatever was going on with Jack.

"Hey. Sorry to disturb your evening. Brandon left me a weird phone message about forty-five minutes ago. I couldn't make out what he was saying, so I drove out here, and the lights are off, nobody is answering, and the door is standing wide open."

"You drove out *where*?"

"To Skull House."

"I'm not following."

What was there not to follow? Ellery thought that given the circumstances, he had given a fairly concise recounting of events. He said—and it's possible his tone was a little elevated, "I think something's wrong! I think something's happened to Brandon!"

"Okay, calm down," Jack said.

Is there ANYTHING more annoying than being told to calm down when you're already doing your best to stay in control?

Ellery shouted, "This isn't the time for calm! This is the time for action! I need help. Are you going to help me or not?"

Jack said curtly, "I'll be there in fifteen minutes."

In fact, it took him seventeen minutes, but who was counting?

Oh, right. Ellery was counting. Every single minute. And with each minute, his tension ratcheted higher and higher.

He got Watson out of the car, put his leash on, and walked him around in front of the house. Even the normally fearless Watson seemed skittish, shying away from the edge of tall, whispering grass, and eventually standing on his stubby hind legs for Ellery to pick him up.

Ellery carried the puppy back to the car, keeping an uneasy eye on the tall, forbidding face of the house. High overhead, the silver eye of the moon peered down from between the gauzy tatters of clouds. Window shutters banged in the night breeze.

When the front door creaked ominously and then slammed shut, Ellery sprinted for the car, jumped inside and locked the door. He gave a shaky laugh and cuddled Watson, who was snuffling into his neck as though they really *had* had a close call.

A moment or two later he saw a red-blue glow, and Jack's SUV crested the hill.

The SUV drew up beside Ellery's VW. Jack got out, the wind whipping his hair in his face. Ellery climbed out, pushing his car door against the gusts that threatened to slam it shut.

"You okay?" Jack asked. "You're not hurt or anything?" The wind blew the words away, but Ellery still heard them. Jack was scowling, but his eyes were dark with concern.

"I'm okay," Ellery said. "But I think something's happened to Brandon."

Jack threw a frowning glance at the dark and silent house. Inside the car, Watson began to bark maniacally, hopping up and down in the driver's seat.

Arf. Arf. Arf.

Jack stared at Ellery. "You brought Watson?"

"Of course I brought Watson. What was I going to do? Tell him to get a room at the Seacrest Inn for the night?"

Ellery was always snappish when he was anxious, and maybe Jack knew that because he said, "Okay, okay. From the top."

Arf. Arf. Arf.

"I told you Brandon and I were supposed to meet for drinks after dress rehearsal. But rehearsal ended early, so I went over to the Salty Dog with everyone for a quick drink to celebrate. And that's when Brandon called. Or that's when I saw he'd left a message. I couldn't make out what he was saying, but I thought I heard the words *house* and *help*."

His hands were shaking as he groped for his phone and handed it over to Jack.

Jack put the phone to his ear, bending his head to better hear, frowning…

How weird was it that with everything going on, Ellery was absurdly conscious of the herbal scent of Jack's aftershave?

ARF. ARF. ARF.

Watson was bouncing against the window like he was playing his own version of handball. Jack threw the pup an exasperated look. "Quiet, you!"

That was sort of charming: Jack's innocent belief that Watson agreed with the concept of law and order.

Watson just barked louder and jumped higher. Jack handed the phone back to Ellery.

"I can't understand a word of that."

"But you can hear from his tone that something's wrong."

"He sounds agitated, I'll give you that." Jack glanced up at the dark house. "The door is closed now. Did you go inside?"

"Me? No."

Jack looked skeptical, and Ellery said, "I didn't go in. The wind slammed the door shut while I was walking Watson."

Jack still wore that unconvinced look, but he said, "Right. You wait here, and I'll have a look for Abbott."

"Okay. Thank you." Ellery leaned against the car in relief.

He watched as Jack strode up to the house, rang the bell, knocked, then opened the door and went inside. He saw a light come on, but it was dim and moving behind the first-floor windows, so he knew Jack had turned on his flashlight.

After a few seconds, the flashlight beam vanished from view.

Minutes passed. Ellery waited tensely. Eventually Watson gave up, quieting and then finally curling up in an aggrieved ball and going to sleep.

Still Jack did not return.

Ellery stopped worrying about what had happened to Brandon and began to worry about what had happened to Jack.

After what felt like half an hour, he ducked his head against the wind and hiked back to the house.

He opened the front door, calling, "Jack? You okay?"

Nothing.

Ellery's alarm shot up another bell or two, and he stepped inside. He turned his phone's flashlight on and panned it slowly around the wide entry hall. A cold feeling washed through him that had nothing to do with the temperature.

The high ceilings were draped in glistening cobwebs. The whitewashed plaster walls were criss-crossed with rough timber—ship's beams? Maybe. That was the case at Captain's Seat. On an island, everything was used and reused until it could no longer be repurposed. Battered furniture. Someone had spray-painted GET OUT in red. The giant words stretched down the length of the wall and trailed across a large oil painting hanging crookedly over the fireplace.

The subject of the portrait was a skeleton clad in pirate's costume. A skeleton parrot sat on the pirate's shoulder. That would be Brandon's contribution to the decor, not something original to the house.

What *was* original to the house was the scattered and mostly broken old furniture: fragile tables with missing legs, velvet-upholstered chairs with the stuffing ripped out, draperies yanked down from the windows, a chandelier pulled clear out of the ceiling and lying smashed on the wooden floor. Was this recent damage, something connected to Brandon's absence? Or had the house been in this terrible state for years?

"Jack?"

Only the wind whispering down the chimney answered, and Ellery had to tamp down his unease. He did not believe in ghosts. He *did* believe in dangerous intruders. He also believed in bubonic plague, and if the mouse droppings dusting every available surface were anything to go by, the house was definitely infested. No wonder Brandon had tried to hit him up for room and board.

Floorboards squeaked beneath his soles as he stepped into the next room. Some kind of a drawing room maybe? Whatever, it was definitely in better shape than the front hall. A cot had been set up near the windows. The silver face of the moon seemed to loom outside, peering in. A sleeping bag was neatly rolled up. There were several boxes and suitcases, all seeming untouched. In the breeze from the open door, a crumpled wad of paper skipped across the floor to land by Ellery's shoe.

He reached down to pick it up, smoothed out the folds to reveal the crude drawing of a skull with a knife through it. LAST WARNING read the words at the top. He sucked in a sharp breath.

"*Don't move!*" a voice cried from behind him.

Which, frankly, is a useless command because when you say DON'T MOVE in that alarming tone of yell, *everyone* moves.

Ellery, of course, moved. He spun around and saw a pirate—sword raised—standing in the doorway.

His gasp probably had enough suction to shift furniture a few inches out of position—he was preparing to shout the house down—but then—

"*Ellery?*"

Because while Ellery's brain registered an actual, er, pirate—he could have *sworn* he saw the eye patch and cruel smile—coming toward him, what he was actually looking at was an original pirate costume on display in a tall glass case next to the door. *Jack* stood in the doorway.

Ellery swallowed his scr—shout—and gulped out, "I-I thought you were a..." His voice died as he realized Jack was pointing a pistol at him.

Even as he recognized—belatedly—the real danger, Jack holstered his pistol. His tone was less alarming and a lot more exasperated as he came to meet Ellery. "You thought what? Why are you in here? I specifically told you to wait outside."

"I know. But when you didn't come back—"

"I told you I was going to search the house."

"After half an hour—"

"It's been ten minutes."

They were now face-to-face, but somehow Ellery kept walking and somehow Jack's arms opened wide, and they were hugging each other.

"Everything's okay," Jack murmured, his breath warm against Ellery's ear. "What did you think?"

Rhetorical question, right? *Bad things.*

"I don't know," Ellery muttered. He felt like a fool, but he hugged Jack all the tighter because for one awful, crazy moment...and because it felt so *good*, so *right* to be in Jack's hard, muscular arms, to feel Jack hugging him back. It had been a long time since anyone hugged him. He hadn't realized how much he missed that simple gesture of comfort.

"God. I could have shot you." Jack sounded genuinely troubled.

"Maybe this place *is* haunted."

They seemed to recall themselves at the same time, letting go, stepping back.

"Did you find him?" Ellery asked. He was dreading the answer, so it was a surprise when Jack shook his head.

"Nope. No sign of him."

"*No?*"

"No. And no sign of foul play."

Foul play? So archaic a term. But sadly, still as relevant as ever.

"But what about the graffiti in the hall? What about this?" Ellery thrust the crumpled paper with its macabre warning toward Jack.

Jack took it, reading it by flashlight. He stared at Ellery. "Where did you find this?"

"It was balled up and blowing around in here."

Jack seemed to consider.

"So, Abbott didn't take it too seriously," he concluded.

"We don't know that."

"He didn't report it. He threw it away. Right?"

"He thought something was wrong. He left me that message. And what about the message in the hallway?"

"That's been there for as long as I've been on the island. There's graffiti all through the house."

Some of Ellery's certainty deflated. And yet, his instinct—no, common sense—told him something was very wrong here.

"But then, where is he?"

"I have no idea. He could be out for a walk. He could have taken a drive. He's a grown man. He's allowed to leave his house if he wants to."

"What about a secret passage?" Ellery asked suddenly. "All these old houses on the island have secret passages and hidden rooms."

"Why would Abbott be hiding in a secret passage?"

"I don't know, but—"

"And how would I find this secret passage, assuming it even exists?"

"I don't know," Ellery admitted.

"Neither do I. I think we have to—"

"His car," Ellery interrupted. "Did you check to make sure—"

Jack said patiently, "Yes. That's what took ten minutes. I walked out to the garage behind the house. His rental car isn't there."

"This doesn't make sense," Ellery protested.

"From what you've told me, Abbott isn't a sensible guy."

"But why would he leave me that message?"

"Ellery." Jack was still striving for patience, but he sounded a little weary. "That message could mean anything. Even you admit you couldn't make out more than a word or two."

"Yes, but one of those words was *help*."

"Which could be a request to come help him paint tomorrow. Or he could be hoping to get this very reaction out of you. Who knows? All I'm sure of is I don't have anything resembling a crime scene, let alone a crime."

Ellery gazed meaningfully at the threatening note Jack held.

Jack said, "For all we know, Nora sent that to him."

"Oh, come on!"

Jack shrugged. "My point still stands. There's no specific threat. We don't even know Abbott is really missing. He could be back any minute."

Ellery shook his head. "I don't think so. I have a bad feeling about this."

"Unfortunately, I can't open an investigation based on someone's bad feeling. And with nothing else to go on, there's not a lot I can do." As Ellery opened his mouth, Jack added, "*Yet.* That doesn't mean I'm going to forget about this, all right? I'll check back with Abbott tomorrow. Make sure he's fine. But I can't do anything more tonight." He studied Ellery. "And neither can you. Understand?"

Reluctantly, Ellery nodded.

"Good. Why don't I walk you to your car so you can go home and get some sleep?"

Well, that was clear enough. Not that Ellery had been thinking they were going to go grab a coffee together. The sidewalks in Pirate's Cove rolled up at nightfall this time of year. He would have liked to have talked this out a little more with Jack. Heck, he'd have liked to talk about anything with Jack.

Ellery nodded again. "Yeah, okay. I do need to get some sleep. Tomorrow will be a long day."

He preceded Jack out of the house. They walked in silence to their vehicles.

As Ellery opened his car door, Jack said suddenly, "Sorry I missed you these last couple of mornings."

"Oh. Right. Well."

Brilliant. With dialogue like that, his future as a screenwriter was assured. But something about Jack's solemn and yet sort of off-hand tone made him self-conscious. He thought Jack looked uncomfortable.

Jack didn't say anything else, so Ellery said, equally off-hand, "Good night." He offered a half-smile and climbed into his car.

Jack had still not started his engine as Ellery's VW trundled over the hill, shutting the house and Jack's SUV's headlights from view.

"That was weird."

Watson muttered and did not bother to raise his head.

"And I don't think I'm imagining it."

This was why he hadn't been in any hurry to get involved after his relationship with Todd had ended. It was too painful when things went wrong. And things always went wrong. Nor did he think it was his fault. There had to be a reason Jack was still available this many years after his wife's death. It's not like he hadn't had plenty of opportunity. He practically had a fan club in Pirate's Cove.

It was telling that Jack had felt it necessary to address not showing up for their usual coffee and chat that morning. And equally telling that he hadn't bothered to come up with an excuse.

Nor had he mentioned stopping by tomorrow. Or coming to see the play.

Whatever. Ellery was not going to fret about it. He had bigger worries than Jack's change of heart. Assuming Jack had a heart.

Regardless of what Jack thought, regardless of a lack of evidence, something *had* happened to Brandon.

Something bad.

CHAPTER EIGHT

He did not sleep well that night.

In Ellery's dreams, the greatcoat-clad skeleton of John Mansfield strode through the cobwebbed halls of Skull House, sword in hand, seeking his prey. Sometimes that prey was Brandon. Sometimes Mansfield *was* Brandon. Sometimes *Ellery* was Brandon. (Frankly, that was worse than the other nightmares put together.)

Each time Ellery woke, gulping and drenched in sweat, he tried to reassure himself that these nightmares were just that: nightmares. But he couldn't quite brush aside the clinging strands of dread and anxiety. Turning the bedside lamp on didn't help. The sight of scorch marks on the wooden panels and door, the faded carpet concealing the hiding place where a blood-stained murder weapon had been found not that long ago, and the bewigged and steely-eyed life-sized portrait of his distant ancestor Captain Horatio Page did nothing to cheer him up.

Why, he asked himself again, had he left the familiarity and safety of the city for Buck Island and Pirate's Cove? There were plenty of other places he could have chosen to make a fresh start. Places where people wouldn't try to kill him or frame him for murder. Places where he wouldn't feel like a fish out of water. As the wind moaned down the chimney, an overwhelming sense of loneliness flooded him. He listened uneasily to the glass rattling in brittle window frames, tree branches scratching against the wall of the house. Even Watson's sleeping whimpers were unnervingly humanlike and troubled.

Ellery blinked at the shadowy ceiling, wondering what had gone wrong. He had been okay a couple of nights ago. He had been happy and hopeful. Even Brandon's sudden reappearance hadn't really shaken him. He hadn't been thrilled about it, but he hadn't felt like *this*. Depressed.

What had changed?

Jack had changed.

Yes. That was part of it. Jack's abrupt and confusing withdrawal. Until Jack had inexplicably retreated, Ellery hadn't realized how much he was starting to, well, care. He had been conscious he didn't want things to develop too quickly—he did not want the pain and drama of another relationship going south—but he had been enjoying their growing friendship, their casual flirtation.

He could not see any reason for Jack to pull back. It wasn't like Ellery had been pushing for more.

Nor did he think Jack had been jealous of Brandon. Jack was neither insecure nor unobservant.

But something had definitely caused Jack to slam on the brakes. Which was doubly frustrating, because Jack was the one who had asked Ellery out. Jack had escalated things. Jack was the one who had said, *"I think it would be nice to see where this goes."*

Well, maybe it had only taken Jack the length of dinner to figure out he wasn't interested in where things with Ellery might go.

Painful to think, but after all, that was how dating worked. You spent time with someone to see if you wanted to spend *more* time with them. Most of the time, in Ellery's experience, the answer was enough was as good as a feast. And according to local gossip, that was certainly Jack's pattern. Or the way things had worked with Sue Lewis.

So. Okay. It was disappointing—more disappointing than Ellery had expected—but it wasn't the end of the world. Not like his heart was broken. Surely, there was no reason he and Jack couldn't go back to being friends, once Jack understood that Ellery wasn't going to be awkward. Wasn't going to pull a Sue Lewis.

Right?

Why then this persistent feeling of unease? Of sadness?

Round and round his thoughts went, like Watson chasing his tail, until finally Ellery fell back into exhausted sleep.

Saturday dawned gray and overcast.

The wind had died down, but instead of leaving the air clear and bright, the morning felt heavy and humid. Oppressive.

He tried phoning Brandon again while he made coffee and toast, but not only did he not reach Brandon, he didn't even get his voice mail. That dead silence on the other end of the phone gave Ellery a sinking sensation. Sure, Brandon could have forgotten to charge his phone. Heck, he could have dropped it down a well. But Ellery didn't believe it. He believed that no reply was significant, if not downright sinister.

He tried to be comforted by the fact that Jack had said there were no signs of foul play, but after all, Jack had been poking around in the near dark. It wasn't as if a forensic team had gone through Skull House.

On what planet was a front door banging open and shut, with no sign of the homeowner anywhere, not a very bad sign?

True, it was sort of reassuring that the vandalism in the entry hall predated Brandon's taking possession of the property, but that crumpled note had not predated Brandon. That had surely been an active threat—and maybe not the first, since it said LAST warning.

Or was that poetic license?

But why warn him at all?

That was the question Ellery kept coming back to. Why would anyone—besides Nora—care that Brandon had taken possession of Skull House?

Other than Nora, and possibly other members of the now defunct historical society, no one else had attempted to purchase the abandoned estate. Sure, real estate was at a premium on the island, but even so. It was not as though that remote location was a sought-after property.

And as het up as Nora had seemed over Brandon snatching the house out from under her, it was impossible to picture her writing threatening notes, let alone doing him actual injury. Nora had her faults, but Ellery believed she was good-hearted and kind.

Not that good-hearted, kind people didn't ever commit murder. Jack had recounted several fairly hair-raising stories about unlikely suspects that had occurred during his time as a homicide detective at LAPD.

Or maybe it wasn't about Brandon taking over the property itself, so much as his writing about the history of the house? Yes, that probably made more sense.

Skull House had a mysterious and murderous history. It was improbable that anyone cared if Brandon wrote about John Mansfield and Ann Rathbone, but Steve Robertson and Rebecca Witherspoon? There was a good chance both murderess and victim still had friends and family in Pirate's Cove.

But really, so what?

If someone was truly set against that twenty-year-old case being reinvestigated, well, that's what lawsuits were for. The town fathers had prevented the filming of a true-crime documentary. Why not take the legal route with Brandon?

Besides, it wasn't like Brandon's investigations into famous cold cases had ever uncovered any previously unknown solution. In Brandon's version of events, the supernatural was always the culprit.

But.

Brandon had said he wanted to enlist Ellery's detective skills. He had hinted that there were dark secrets to be uncovered in Pirate's Cove. Maybe, as unlikely as it seemed, Brandon *had* really intended to investigate Steve Robertson's murder.

Except... What was there to investigate? It was common knowledge Rebecca Witherspoon had killed her harasser. No, wait. There *was* a mystery. The mystery of what had happened to Rebecca. Had she jumped into the sea like her legendary ancestress? Or had she escaped?

If Rebecca had escaped, there was no way she had returned to Pirate's Cove. She'd be living in Alaska. Or Greenland. Certainly, she'd be as far as she could get from Buck Island. The idea of Rebecca Witherspoon striking down Brandon to prevent his nosing around the past was pretty far-fetched.

All of this was pretty far-fetched.

And yet, *something* had happened to Brandon. Either he had driven away of his own volition and was refusing to answer phone calls, *or* someone had made him disappear.

* * * * *

"Did you know Rebecca Witherspoon?" Ellery asked Nora.

They were having lunch in the Crow's Nest. Nora had made her "secret family recipe" clam chowder, and she spilled a few milky drops as Ellery asked his question.

"Why would you ask that, dearie?"

"I just wondered. You've lived on the island forever. I thought you might have some insight."

Nora was staring at him. "Insight into what? Who's been talking to you?"

Her reaction was so unexpected, Ellery asked, "Is there some reason people *shouldn't* talk to me?"

Something flickered in Nora's gray gaze. She turned her attention to her soup. "No. Of course not. But it's old news. Sad news. People don't like to speak of it much, that's all."

"I guess that makes sense." Ellery spooned up a mouthful of creamy chowder. He knew Nora's love of gossip and was pretty sure she'd be unable to leave the conversation there.

Sure enough, after a moment or two, Nora said, "Brandon Abbott is poking his nose in, I suppose. I never believed for a moment he was only writing about John Mansfield and Ann Rathbone."

"Pretty unlikely," Ellery agreed. "He'll probably tie the two crimes together and have the ghost of Ann Rathbone murdering Steve Robertson."

Nora snorted. "Probably."

Ellery considered telling Nora he believed Brandon was missing. Of course, officially, Brandon wasn't missing. Not yet. As far as Ellery knew, he was the only person in town who even suspected such a thing. He was going to feel like an idiot if Brandon suddenly showed up.

In any case, Nora was still following her own thoughts. "I knew them both. Becky helped out summers at the historical society. She had many interests. She was part of the diving club, the drama club, the debate club. She was a lovely girl. Pretty. Smart. Not popular. Or, I should say, not one of the in-crowd. She knew what she wanted. She had a bright future ahead of her."

Ellery mulled over what "in-crowd" meant in modern terms. "She had gone away to college but was back for spring break?"

"That's right. She was studying archeology."

"What about Steve? Did he help out at the historical society too?"

"Steve Robertson?" Nora shook her head at the idea. "That boy never had a thought in his head for anything older than himself."

"Other or older?"

"Older."

An important distinction? "Were he and Rebecca a couple?"

Nora hesitated. "I don't think so. I don't know. Becky wasn't a girl to spend her days babbling about boys."

Or maybe she had saved the boy babble for her friends and not a much older coworker?

Nora added, "They did have some kind of chemistry, I'll admit that."

"Becky and Steve?"

"Yes. They irritated each other, but I think there was attraction there as well." Her expression grew briefly melancholy.

"Do their families still live on the island?"

"Steve's mother still lives in Pirate's Cove. His father died a few years ago. Becky's parents moved off island a few months after the...the murder."

"Hmm..."

Nora easily followed his thoughts. She shook her head. "No. Becky didn't run to them. They were both killed in a car crash about a year later." She sighed. "I don't believe Becky ever left the island. I don't think she survived that night. I don't know what happened. Drink. Drugs. Something terrible."

Something terrible, for sure. It wouldn't have been the first time in the history of the world that a party had gotten out of control with tragic consequences.

"But would she really have jumped into the ocean like Ann Rathbone? Do girls really do stuff like that nowadays?"

Nora was silent. She said finally, "I didn't believe it at first. But now..."

"Now you do? You think she took her own life?"

"She was a romantic. Not about boys, but about the past, about history. Especially the history of Buck Island. She knew the stories and legends of this island nearly as well as I do. I think if she was in a fragile state—and she would have been, wouldn't she?—yes, I think she might have followed her ancestor to a watery grave."

* * * * *

"Is that so?" drawled Libby in character as Lily Montaigne. She tossed her head, and her blonde wig slipped ever so slightly left. She casually righted it. "You're a great man, Inspector Wetherell, but you're losing your grip. I was locked in a cell at Havre de Grace at the very moment you accuse me of committing this murder!"

Cyrus, portraying Inspector Wetherell, chuckled like a Vaudeville villain. If he'd had a mustache, he'd no doubt be twirling it. Apparently, he still didn't realize Wetherell was the good guy. "That had me stumped for a time, Lily. And yet the answer was so simple. Daylight Saving Time! When it was eight-five in Havre de Grace, it was nine-five here in Delaware."

The audience roared with laughter.

Ellery, scrunched down in the front row, resisted the temptation to crawl under his seat.

"*Lily!*" gasped Felix. He was playing Marc Morales—and very well too. He was the one member of the Scallywags who made you believe he was someone else. "It's not true! Tell them it's not true."

This was *excruciating*. Why had he ever let Dylan talk him into adapting his screenplay for the stage? And why had he ever thought turning the play into a historical was a good idea?

Okay, he knew the answer to the last one. When he had asked Jack about some finer points of police procedure, Jack had been merciless. Jack had said Ellery had set police procedures back about a century, and Ellery had boldly decided to go with that.

Which maybe wasn't the worst idea he'd ever had, because all that stagy dialogue would have sounded even worse in a contemporary setting.

As it was... Ouch.

Speaking of Jack, he had not made it to opening night. Granted, it was like Jack to work so that other members of his team could attend the play, but Ellery couldn't help feeling Jack's absence was pointed.

Cyrus was delivering his theatrical coup de grâce. "After I made inquiries, I discovered Maryland had remained on Standard Time all summer. Which means you had nearly an hour to get from Wilmington to Havre de Grace after you killed Nick Donnelly. Ample time for a speeder like you!"

The audience burst into laughter again, and there were hoots of "He's got you, Libby!" from the peanut gallery.

Ellery moaned softly. Sandy Morita, who ran the small art gallery on the other side of the Crow's Nest, patted his hand. She was giggling.

At last, AT LAST, the torture ended, and the audience jumped to their feet, delivering thunderous applause for cast and crew. The cast came out for several bows, and finally Dylan took the stage and summoned Ellery.

Ellery climbed the steps to the brightly lit stage in response to cries of "Author! Author!"

"Didn't I tell you?" Dylan was beaming as he handed Ellery the mic.

Ellery took the mic, gazing at the laughing faces of the still standing audience. As the clapping subsided and people took their seats, he said, "Good evening. I'm so glad you all could join us tonight. This play has been a long time in the making, and the cast and crew worked their butts off for tonight's, er, result."

The audience clapped and laughed again. Dylan chuckled and slapped him on the back.

"So be sure to tell all your friends—if any of them aren't here tonight—and thank you again for your support!"

The music began to play, the curtain lowered, and Ellery turned to Dylan.

"Brilliant!" Dylan exclaimed. Ellery reached to strangle him, and Dylan batted his hands away. "Never mind that now. We're a hit!"

That did seem to be the backstage consensus.

The response to *Murder Mansion* had exceeded everyone's expectations. The fact that the audience believed it was a comedy and Ellery had written it to be a serious murder mystery did not seem to worry anyone else, so Ellery tried to be stoic about it. Better to be hailed a comic genius in France—or Rhode Island—than known for the literary goof you really were, right?

The meet and greet in the theater lobby was actually fun—the generous quantities of circulating champagne no doubt helped—and then everyone changed into their street clothes to head for the Salty Dog.

No Jack in the pub either, so he probably *was* working that night. Which was a relief, even though Ellery told himself he didn't care one way or the other.

He was more than ready for a real drink. He ordered his favorite Upside-Down Pirate and settled back to enjoy the celebration.

At the pub, person after person came up to congratulate them. Libby received more roses from her father and Felix. A couple of patrons bought the whole table a round of drinks.

Mid-festivities, Officer Martin came in and asked to speak to Cyrus. Cyrus looked surprised, then concerned, and went outside.

"I wonder what that's about," Dylan said.

Ellery barely heard him. Sick apprehension pooled in his gut. He noticed the raucous noise level within the pub had grown muted. Hilarity was replaced with hushed voices and whispering. He was pretty sure he wasn't imagining that people were looking his way. Not at the crowded table. At *him*.

Cyrus came back inside. His cheery countenance was uncharacteristically grave. He glanced around the table, spotted Ellery, came toward him with seemingly reluctant steps.

"Ellery, my boy, might I have a word?"

His throat felt bone dry. Too dry for words. Ellery nodded, rose, followed the mayor outside the pub.

The night was stingingly cold for June, but Ellery barely noticed.

Cyrus, an unwholesome shade of yellow in the light from the pub windows, cleared his throat. "Ellery, I'm afraid I have some bad news."

"Go on."

He knew what Cyrus was going to say. He had been expecting this since the night before. And yet it still felt unreal as Cyrus said in a strained, hushed voice, "It's your friend. Your...your ex-boyfriend. I'm sorry. They found his body a few hours ago."

CHAPTER NINE

"Where?"

That must not have been the response Cyrus expected, because he blinked, said cautiously, "The men renovating Skull House discovered him dead on the rocks below the house."

"How did it happen?"

"Oh. Er, I don't think they're quite sure yet. Or at least, Police Chief Carson isn't sharing that information. Presumably the town council will be briefed in due course." He added, "I'm sure it was an accident."

"Right." Ellery listened numbly. He was thinking that Brandon must have been lying dead on the beach all the while he had been walking Watson, all the time he and Jack had been exploring Skull House, lying there in the moonlight when he and Jack had driven away. He felt shocked, stricken. He felt afraid. Because regardless of what the mayor believed, Brandon's death could not be an accident. Even without knowing the details, he was certain of that much: Brandon had been murdered.

It didn't sound like everyone had reached that conclusion, though. Certainly, the mayor did not seem concerned with anything beyond Ellery's feelings. Which was kind, of course, but Ellery felt miscast in the role of bereaved.

"The house should never have been sold," Cyrus said. "It should have been torn down years ago. It should have been torn down after—" He broke off, saying instead, "I blame myself."

"But you couldn't have stopped the sale, could you?"

"Well, no," Cyrus admitted. "I used to think sometimes that the town council ought to try to purchase the property, but it's too far from the village to be any kind of practical investment." He sighed. "Even the Buck Island Conservancy wasn't willing to take it off the Tideworth family's hands."

Ellery nodded. He wasn't really listening, wasn't even sure why he had asked the question.

Watching him, Cyrus said kindly, "Is there anything I can do? Anything you need, dear boy?"

"No." Ellery shook his head. "It's just hard to take in."

"I had the impression that you and Abbott weren't particularly close, but of course…"

"We weren't close." Ellery shivered. "I think I'll grab my jacket and head home. Unless… Does Jack— do the police want to talk to me?"

"Young Martin didn't say so. I'm sure Chief Carson will contact you when he's concluded his... his preliminary investigation."

"Yes. Thanks, Mayor." Ellery pushed open the door and went back inside the pub. Cyrus followed.

"What's up?" Dylan asked as Ellery opened his wallet and threw a couple of bills on the table.

"Brandon. His contractors found him dead on the beach below Skull House."

"Oh my God."

There were gasps up and down the table, followed by questions that neither Ellery nor Cyrus could answer.

"When?" Nora asked. "When did it happen? Had demolition begun inside the house?"

Ellery moved his head in negation. He hadn't seen signs of demolition, but it had been dark and he hadn't got very far in the house.

"Let me know if there's anything I can do." Dylan spoke in an under voice.

"Thanks. I will." Ellery shrugged into his jacket, raised his hand in brief good night, and left the pub.

* * * * *

Sundays were Ellery's day off.

Okay, *off* was comparative, because he typically spent his Sundays working his tail off on a variety of DIY projects around Captain's Seat. With Jack's help he had managed to rip up the gungy green linoleum in the kitchen and replace it with black and teal polished concrete. With Jack's help he had painted the dining room an elegant shade of ivory. With Jack's—well, never mind. Jack's help was clearly a thing of the past. Moving forward, Ellery would be handling the home improvement projects on his own.

But not today.

He had slept badly—when he had slept at all—and woke tired and worried.

He couldn't help feeling uneasy that Jack had left it to Mayor Jones to inform him of Brandon's death. Of course, Jack would be busy with the investigation, and he knew Ellery did not still have tender feelings for his ex, but still. Having been on the suspecto numero uno side of one homicide investigation, Ellery had no desire to repeat the experience. He was very much aware he was the only person in Pirate's Cove who had any kind of history with Brandon. Who might conceivably have a motive for getting Brandon out of the way.

There was nothing Ellery would like more than to be able to convince himself Brandon's death had been accidental, but how could it be?

It was just too much of a coincidence that Brandon had started poking around in the mystery of Steve Robertson's murder, and now Brandon was dead too.

And what about that *Last Warning* note? The note Jack had confiscated without seeming to take it at all seriously.

Unsurprising, then, that Ellery wasn't feeling particularly productive. Thank goodness for Watson. Not only did tending to the puppy's needs force routine, if not actual structure, but Watson's energetic, playful personality created a positive, happy energy in the empty old house. It was impossible not to smile as he watched Watson chasing a plastic wiffle ball around the legs of the kitchen table.

Ellery fed Watson, then checked his messages—his cell phone seemed ominously silent. He made coffee and carried it out to the terrace behind the house, settling at the china pink marble table and chairs.

He drank his coffee and watched Watson trotting around the garden, chasing butterflies, barking at birds, then scooting back to sit on Ellery's feet when something startled him.

"You're okay," he told Watson, and Watson's ears flicked. He settled his furry little bottom more firmly in Ellery's foot.

"Everything's okay," Jack had said, and in that moment, Ellery had believed him.

He thought about weeding the rose beds. He thought about pruning the hedges. He thought about mowing what was left of the grass. He did none of those things. He realized he was waiting for the other shoe to drop, and shortly before noon, drop it did.

Ellery's cell rang, and Jack's name flashed up. Ellery felt a wave of relief—followed by a flare of wariness. He pressed Accept and said crisply, "This is Ellery."

"Ellery, it's Chief Carson."

Ellery's unease only grew at Jack's formal tone. "Noted."

There was a hesitation before Jack said awkwardly, "I'm sure you've heard the news by now."

"Yes. Cyrus filled me in last night. Not that he had much information beyond the fact that Brandon is dead." It was all he could do not to add an accusatory, *Like I told you!* It wasn't Jack's fault Brandon was dead.

Maybe Jack heard all that he wasn't saying. He sighed. "Look, I'd like you to come down to the station. We need to go over a few things."

Was he being paranoid? Ellery wanted to think so, but his instinctive reaction was a strong Talk to the Hand.

"What things? What's going on?"

"We can discuss that when you get here," Jack said in that clipped, no-nonsense tone Ellery hadn't heard since the Maples homicide investigation.

"Do I need to phone my lawyer?"

He was mostly being a smartass, so it was a shock when Jack shot back, "Maybe. Do you have a lawyer?"

After a stunned moment, Ellery said, "I guess I'll phone one now. I sure won't be answering your questions without one present."

"Ellery, wait." Jack sounded more like his normal self. Or at least his normal exasperated self.

"Let's not escalate this. You know we have to ask about your relationship with Abbott."

"I've already told you everything there is to know, Jack."

"On the record. Officially."

Ellery was silent. He did know that. But along with considerable alarm, Jack's manner and tone had triggered unexpected resentment and hostility.

"It's important to get this right," Jack added, which was cryptic but convincing.

Ellery said tersely, "All right. I'll be there shortly."

Jack hung up without another word.

*　*　*　*　*

If a police station could be cozy, Pirate's Cove PD had a cozy little hoosegow. Sure, the windows were bulletproof and the officers were armed, but there were a lot of potted plants on desks and finger paintings on bulletin boards. The coffee wasn't bad, and there was a never-ending supply of baked goods in the "coffee corner." Ellery happened to know the nosh was financed by the chief himself.

Ellery seemed to be expected because no sooner did he arrive at the front desk, than baby-faced Officer Martin jumped up and led him back to Jack's office. Martin rapped on the door, Jack's pleasant voice bade him enter, and Martin shoved the door open.

"Mr. Page is here, Chief."

Jack beckoned, and Ellery stepped inside the office. The door closed behind him.

A dark-haired, thin-faced man Ellery did not recognize sat in front of Jack's desk. The man eyed him with cool gray eyes. Both he and Jack were dressed in jeans and navy polo shirts marked PC POLICE.

They were probably not being ironic.

"Thanks for coming in, Ellery." Jack pointed to the other empty chair in front of his desk.

Ellery took the indicated seat. He thought Jack looked tired. He needed a shave, and there were dark shadows beneath his blue-green eyes.

"This is Detective Lansing," Jack informed him. "He's working the Abbott case."

Wait. What? Since when did Pirate's Cove have a dedicated detective on the rolls? In Ellery's experience, Jack's uniformed officers worked every case with Jack taking lead on any real detecting required. They were a small force policing a small community. The RI State Police provided any additional backup.

He nodded politely at Detective Lansing.

Detective Lansing didn't waste any time. "Mr. Page, the chief has given me his account of your Friday night visit to the property known as Skull House. I'd like to get your version of events."

In fairness, Lansing was scrupulously neutral in tone and words. In fact, it was something about that uberscrupulous impersonality that put Ellery's back up. Not that his back could get much higher. By then, his psychic image probably resembled a Halloween black-cat cartoon.

Ellery related the events of Friday evening. The phone call he had received while out celebrating a successful dress rehearsal, his drive to Skull House, his discovery of the open door and subsequent concern, and his summoning of Chief Carson.

He played the phone message for Detective Lansing. Lansing listened to the static-laced recording without emotion. He shrugged. "Personally, I couldn't swear to what was said, but apparently you heard something alarming enough to cause you to immediately leave the party and drive through the night to see what was happening with your ex."

Ellery opened his mouth to say that Brandon had not been his ex, but of course that was exactly what Brandon was. It was just the way Detective Lansing said the word *ex*; the emphasis he put on that tiny syllable made it sound so much more significant. As though Brandon wasn't an ex at all. As though their relationship was current and ongoing.

"Yes."

That was probably a little terse. But in the weeks since Ellery had been suspected of killing Trevor Maples, he'd read a lot of mystery novels, and he had learned that saying as little as possible to the police was always a best practice.

"That's very interesting," Lansing said, "given that Abbott phoned you at 4:45 Friday afternoon."

"*What?*" Ellery glanced quickly from Lansing to Jack. Jack gazed back at him, and it was immediately clear to Ellery that this was not news to him. "No. That's not right. I only—" He stopped mid word.

"You were saying?" Lansing asked with fake courtesy.

Ellery's heart began to thump with a mixture of fright and fury. "My phone was on Do Not Disturb during the rehearsal. I turned it off when I walked into the theater and didn't remember to turn it on again until I was sitting in the Salty Dog. I never noticed the time stamp. I just noticed that I'd received a message."

"You turned off your phone for the entire evening?" Lansing asked skeptically.

"Yes. Of course I did! It was the dress rehearsal. We all turned our phones off."

Jack and Lansing glanced at each other.

"We'll leave that for now," Lansing said. "Mr. Page, I'm not going to beat about the bush. Your former boyfriend was murdered."

"Murdered," Ellery repeated slowly. Even though he had been expecting this, hearing the words out loud was still shocking.

"That's right. We're investigating Brandon Abbott's death as a homicide."

"How was he…killed?"

"We won't know for sure until we've received the full autopsy report."

"Are you *sure* he was murdered?"

Jack and Detective Lansing shared another of those indecipherable looks. Detective Lansing said sardonically, "Yes, Mr. Page, we're sure."

That time Ellery said nothing.

"So you can understand why we're so eager to hear the full story. By your own account, you're very likely the last person to speak to the victim."

"You've already heard the full story," Ellery said. He leveled a stony look at Jack. Jack's lashes lowered, veiling his gaze.

"We want to know exactly what happened from the moment you arrived at Skull House."

"I already told you exactly what happened not five minutes ago. How many times do I have to go through it?"

Jack said wearily, "As many times as it takes."

Once again, Ellery went through everything he had done from the moment he had received Brandon's phone call."

"You didn't walk to the edge of the cliff and look down? Seems an obvious thing to have done," Lansing said.

"Really?" Ellery said. "Because it didn't occur to Chief Carson either."

Jack cleared his throat.

Lansing said, "We're interested in *your* movements, Mr. Page. Are you sure you didn't go inside the house before Chief Carson arrived? You were concerned enough to drive out there in the middle of the night. It would have been understandable to go inside and see if Abbott had maybe fallen down the stairs."

"I didn't go inside the house. I didn't walk out to the edge of the bluffs. I phoned Jack and told him I thought something might have happened to Brandon."

Lansing's dark eyes flickered at "Jack," but he said, "Okay. What did you think might have happened? What's your theory? Why would someone want to kill your ex?"

"I don't know. I don't have a theory." Something about the blank slate of Jack's expression spurred Ellery to add, "Earlier in the week, Chief Carson seemed to think Brandon's interest in the old Steve Robertson murder might stir up trouble."

Lansing didn't bat an eye. "Yep. Chief Carson and I have discussed that theory."

"Well? It makes sense to me. I can't think of any other reason someone might want Brandon out of the way."

"No?"

"No."

"You don't see why you might be a person of interest in this investigation?"

Ellery stared. "What does *that* mean?"

"Person of interest? It means you're a suspect. In fact, you're our number-one suspect."

Ellery ignored the sarcasm, if it was sarcasm. "*Why?*" Really, none of this made sense to him.

"Well, to start with, you're the only person on this island who knew Abbott. You not only knew him, you had a contentious relationship with him."

"Thanks, friend," Ellery said bitterly to Jack.

Jack's light gaze flickered, but he did not speak.

"In fact"—Lansing leaned forward to emphasize his point—"you had a confrontation with Abbott the very morning of his death. There are witnesses to words being exchanged in your bookshop."

Déjà vu. Hadn't he just been through this a few weeks earlier?

"Words are always exchanged in a bookshop. That's what a bookshop is. A marketplace for words."

"Ellery," Jack said in warning.

"Jack, this is *ridiculous*," Ellery protested. "I can't believe you think I'm a suspect. Because I argued with Brandon? You know I hadn't seen him in years. *Why* would I suddenly decide to kill him? It's crazy."

Lansing said, "Now calm down, Mr. Page. We have to ask these questions. We're just doing our job."

Ellery shook his head. This didn't feel routine to him.

"I guess if all we had to go on was the fact that you used to be tight with Abbott and you argued with him the morning he died, you'd be right in wondering why we're focusing so much attention on you. But I think you know there's something else that might raise a suspicion or two. It's not something you'd forget."

Ellery didn't try to hide his bewilderment. "I have zero clue what you're talking about."

"Come on." Lansing grinned with weirdly friendly mockery. "Are you saying you don't know about the will?"

Ellery's heart stopped. He felt the blood drain from his face. "What will?"

"The will where your former boyfriend leaves you all his money, all his property, and his entire literary estate."

CHAPTER TEN

He fully expected them to arrest him then and there—and strangely, he could think of nothing to say.

Ellery looked at Lansing. He looked at Jack. He looked back at Lansing. He swallowed, a sound that came out more like an audible gulp in the small office.

"You didn't know," Jack said. Was it Ellery's imagination, or was his tone tinged with relief?

Lansing made a scornful sound. Too irritated for the laugh he intended. "You knew," he said, but he didn't sound quite convinced.

"I *didn't* know." Ellery was speaking to Jack. "I didn't have any idea. Why would he do that?" Not that he expected Jack to have an answer, nor did Jack try to come up with one.

"You *had* to know," Detective Lansing insisted.

Ellery ignored him. "I told you what my relationship with Brandon was like," he said to Jack. To his relief, his voice stayed steady, but that was part of the unfairness of this interview. Interview? *Ha.* Interrogation. He had confided in Jack. Jack the guy who had asked him out, not Jack the police chief.

"Yes," Jack said. "You did."

"I had no reason to think he'd put me in his will. He's sure as heck not in *my* will."

Lansing opened his mouth, but Jack spoke over him.

"All right," Jack said. His tone was brusque. "I think that's it for now. Thanks for coming in, Ellery. We appreciate your cooperation."

Detective Lansing threw Jack a look of disbelief. To Ellery, Lansing said quickly, "We'll be in touch!"

Ellery rose and walked out of the Jack's office without another word. His knees felt wobbly with relief. He had been sure he was going to be arrested. In all honesty, he was amazed he hadn't been. Heck, he probably *did* look like the most likely suspect. He was the only person on the island who really knew Brandon, the only person with a concrete motive, and he had even gone to Brandon's house on what seemed to be the night of the murder.

All the same, he was shaken—and bitterly hurt—by what felt like Jack's betrayal. It was one thing if Jack didn't want to pursue a closer relationship. Fair enough. But for Jack to use in the course of a criminal investigation the information Ellery had shared in confidence? No bueno.

From now on, any conversations Ellery had with Jack would be held with his attorney present. And that went double for any conversations with Detective Lansing.

* * * * *

After parking behind the Crow's Nest, Ellery headed back to the bookstore, passing the newspaper rack in front of the Toy Chest. The banner headline blazing across the front page of the *Scuttlebutt Weekly* caught his eye. He lurched to a horrified stop.

THE USUAL SUSPECT? LOCAL BOOKSELLER NAMED PERSON OF INTEREST IN BRUTAL MURDER!

Ellery patted his pockets for change, found two quarters, and yanked out the paper, his gaze racing across every damning sentence in the article.

Detective George Lansing with PCPD revealed early Sunday morning that the prime suspect in the vicious slaying of local literary celebrity Brandon Abbott is none other than notorious newcomer and New York City transplant Ellery Page. Page, a former bit-part actor and owner of the financially challenged Crow's Nest bookshop, is no stranger to playing a starring role in homicide investigations. This is the second time in four months local law enforcement has identified Page as a prime suspect...

Yada, yada, yada.

Ellery didn't have to check the byline to recognize another one of Sue Lewis's hatchet jobs.

"What is your *problem*?" he demanded, startling a pair of summer-clad shoppers. He waved a quick apology that was part shooing motion, and the ladies hastily dived into Sandy's art gallery.

Of course, by now Ellery had a pretty good idea what Sue's problem was. But Sue was barking up the wrong tree if she believed Ellery was a rival for Jack's affections. That had been illustrated in black and white for Ellery only a few minutes earlier.

He turned the page, nearly tearing it in his haste, and made a sound of disbelief as he saw Sue's review of *Murder Mansion* right next to the rest of her report on Brandon's murder. Seriously? She was critiquing a play she was performing in? Well, at least she gave it a rave review.

He returned to her account of Brandon's death, but it was clear that, aside from her just-short-of-libelous campaign against him, she didn't have much of a story. Brandon's lifeless body had been found beneath the bluffs of Skull House. Cause of death had not yet been verified, but PCPD was treating the death as suspicious.

The victim had first been noticed missing on Friday night when the previously mentioned suspicious character Ellery Page claimed to have been summoned to Skull House. Page had summoned Police Chief Jack Carson to the scene. Chief Carson was currently Unavailable For Comment.

Which was reasonable but sounded dubious.

That was pretty much it. There was no mention of Ellery being named in Brandon's will and no details on who or how Brandon's body had been discovered. There was plenty of background information on Brandon and his writing career, as well as Sue's bewailing the loss to the community that Brandon's death posed.

The one piece of genuine news, in Ellery's opinion, was that Brandon's rental car had been ferried back to the mainland early on the afternoon of his death. It seemed like that might be significant, though he wasn't sure how.

Ellery tossed the newspaper into a nearby trash receptacle and strode into the Crow's Nest, calling, *"Nora!"* He checked mid-stride when he saw her behind the counter, ringing up books for Mrs. Nelson.

Nora jumped guiltily, the cash register dinged, and the drawer shot open.

She hastily slammed the drawer shut. "It wasn't me, Ellery! I give you my word of honor." She put her hand up like a witness swearing to tell the truth, the whole truth, and nothing but the truth before taking the stand. Hopefully it would never come to that.

"It wasn't Nora," Mrs. Nelson intervened. "Jane was the one telling everyone about your argument Friday morning with Brandon Abbott."

"I swear I never said a word." Nora's eyes shone with emotion.

Ellery had been so sure Nora's gossiping had once more gotten him into hot water, he didn't know what to say. He had completely forgotten Mrs. Smith had been in the bookshop that morning.

Mrs. Nelson said grimly, "Jane Smith is a fool. Was it bad? Did they give you the third degree?"

"How did you know I was—" Ellery stopped. *Of course* they knew he was being interviewed by the police. They had probably known he was going to be interviewed before he had.

"Bad enough."

Nora and Mrs. Nelson looked at each other and shook their heads.

"I'm sorry for yelling," Ellery told Nora. "I shouldn't have jumped to conclusions."

"It's a reasonable conclusion," Mrs. Nelson said, and Nora grimaced in acknowledgment.

Yeah, it kinda was. But still unfair. Ellery sighed. "How's business today?"

"Oh, you know," Nora said vaguely, apparently afraid to give him any more bad news.

"Ellery, Nora has had one of her ideas. A particularly brilliant one," Mrs. Nelson said.

"Wellllll," Nora said quickly. "Perhaps now isn't the m—"

"Nonsense. Now is the perfect moment. His morale needs boosting."

Ellery opened his mouth to assure them his morale was perfectly fine flatlined, but Mrs. Nelson didn't give him a chance. "Nora has suggested that we band together with Mr. Starling and yourself to solve Brandon Abbott's murder."

Ellery gaped at them. "*What?*"

"Who better to lead the investigation than our own Miss Marple?"

Nora, beet-red and nearly squirming with discomfort, murmured, "That might be a little..."

"Much?" suggested Ellery. "Ya think?"

Mrs. Nelson ignored them both. "We must move swiftly to circumvent a great miscarriage of justice. No one is better equipped to take on such an endeavor than the Silver Sleuths Book Club."

"I'm thinking the police are better equipped," Ellery said.

Nora shook her head. "No, dearie. There, you're wrong. The police think *you* killed Abbott. Not Chief Carson, of course, but he'll have to recuse himself from the actual investigation, which means—"

"When you want a thing done right, you have to do it yourself," Mrs. Nelson said.

"I appreciate what you're trying to do," Ellery said. "Really. But I don't think this is the way to go. For one thing, if whoever killed Brandon figures out that you're snooping around, it could be..."

"Dangerous. Yes," Nora said crisply. "We realize that."

Ellery was silent. On the one hand, he was touched by their loyalty and faith in him. He wasn't so sure Jack knew he wasn't guilty. And it was painfully clear Sue Lewis was going to use her editorial soapbox to stir up suspicion and doubt again. As much as he wanted to believe the citizens of Pirate's Cove knew him better now and wouldn't be so quick to jump to conclusions, he had the sinking feeling most people were going to think turning up as the prime suspect in *two* murder investigations looked like too much of a coincidence.

"You can't do it on your own," Nora said. "You're going to need backup."

"I..." The truth was he hadn't even got around to thinking what to do to protect himself beyond hiring a lawyer. But yes, this—well, not *this*—but it did make sense that he should examine the circumstances of Brandon's murder, given that he had actually *known* Brandon.

"Now, Nora and I have been considering the victimology, and we're convinced—"

"*Victimology?*" Ellery interrupted.

"Of course, dearie," Nora said kindly. "The investigation must always begin with the victim."

"I know *that*, but..."

Mrs. Nelson continued briskly, "We're convinced that the roots of this crime stretch all the way back to Steve Robertson's murder."

Why stop there? Why not drag John Mansfield and Ann Rathbone into it? But of course, Ellery didn't say that. He too believed Brandon's decision to dredge up Steve Robertson's murder had led to his own.

"There isn't much mystery about Robertson's murder, is there? Was there any doubt that the Witherspoon girl killed him?"

"Of course! No one saw her do it, after all. She wasn't around to question after the fact."

Nora said, "There's always the possibility she could have witnessed the crime and fled."

"But wouldn't she eventually have come forward?" Ellery asked. "I mean, in all these years?"

"Not necessarily. Not if she feared no one would believe her. There's no statute of limitations on murder."

"No one would believe her." Mrs. Nelson's tone brooked no argument. "She was the only one with any motive."

"But I thought you said there was doubt—" Ellery's head was already starting to spin.

"Now *that*, we don't know for sure." Nora's objection was directed at Mrs. Nelson. "That's why we must proceed as if the case had just landed on our desk."

"True, true," Mrs. Nelson conceded.

Ellery said, "It's always possible Brandon's murder has nothing to do with the past. His work attracted some peculiar personalities. We didn't keep in touch, but I remember reading in *Variety* that he'd had to file a restraining order against a fan who turned into a stalker."

"That's a good point," Nora said. "We have to keep an open mind. Which is why we're agreed that you should handle the investigation into Brandon's background, both his personal and professional life. Hermione and I will take point on the Pirate's Cove angle. We thought we would start with Mariah Robertson, Steve's mother. She still lives in the village. Mr. Starling w—"

"Uh, no, you won't," Ellery broke in. "No way. Not a chance in hel-ck."

Their faces fell. They protested in chorus, "Oh, but—"

"You told me you understood that this could be dangerous."

"We do!" Nora said.

"Then you get why I'm going to be the one doing any interviews, especially with anyone on this island."

"Hmm. He may be right," Mrs. Nelson said.

Ellery snorted. "Thanks."

"But you won't know what questions to ask," Nora said. "You won't know who to interview. It would be so much faster if we handled this."

"Yeah, I don't think so. You two can make me a list of who you think I should interview, and you can tell me what you think I ought to ask, but I'll do the actual talking."

He couldn't believe he was agreeing to this. Frankly, he wanted nothing more than to return to Captain's Seat, bar the doors, pull the curtains, pour himself a stiff drink—or two—and hide from the world for a few days. But he might not have a few days to squander on feeling sorry for himself. Nora and Mrs. Nelson were right. The police had definitely set their sights on him. In fact, Detective Lansing seemed to think he had the case all but wrapped up.

And Jack...

This was what hurt the most. Ellery knew Nora and Mrs. Nelson were right about Jack having to recuse himself from investigating Ellery's possible involvement in Brandon's death, but Jack hadn't just been neutral. He could have warned Ellery of what was waiting for him at the station. He had chosen not to. He had let Ellery walk right into that interrogation without so much as a heads-up.

And what felt especially unfair was that Ellery was the one who had been insisting on Friday night that something must have happened to Brandon. Jack had brushed his concerns aside. Had that made a difference to Brandon's survival? Maybe not, but the fact remained: Ellery had alerted the authorities, had tried to get help, and had essentially been told to go home and not worry his pretty little head about it.

So yes, he felt misjudged and hurt and angry. But giving in to those feelings was a luxury he didn't have. Far more satisfying to prove himself innocent, direct the police to the real culprit, and tell Jack to take a hike when he came crawling.

Okay, yes, total fantasy—the last part in particular—but balm to his ego nonetheless.

"Very well," Nora said, snapping him out of his reflections. "If you're determined, then we'd better not waste any more time arguing about it. We're very likely racing the clock."

Mrs. Nelson pushed a yellow legal pad covered in blue scribbles of notes down the counter to Ellery. "Mrs. Robertson lives on Cutty Sark Road."

Ellery's heart did a swan dive. "You want me to go talk to her *now*?"

"Of course!"

"The sooner, the better," Nora said.

"Right. Well." He picked up the legal pad and tried to make sense of Mrs. Nelson's notes. With all the arrows and... Were those thought bubbles? Clouds? Was he even looking at the pad right-side up?

"If you have any questions, you can phone us," Nora said.

"Now you're being funny."

Nora and Mrs. Nelson exchanged surprised looks.

"There's nothing funny about this situation," Mrs. Nelson said.

Ellery muttered, "You're telling me." But he picked up the pad and headed for the door. "I'll be in touch."

CHAPTER ELEVEN

"I know you," Mariah Robertson said wonderingly when she opened her front door to Ellery.

Ellery braced for anything from an accusation of murder to having the peacock-blue door slammed in his face, but Mariah added, "You wrote last night's play. It was very funny."

Last night seemed a million years ago. Ellery offered a weak smile. "Guilty!"

Mariah smiled vaguely. She was small and frail-looking. A faded woman in her late sixties, which surprised Ellery. He had been expecting someone much older. But why? She had probably been about forty when her son had died. Mariah's hair was a washed-out, indeterminate beige, and her eyes were the color of the sky when it had yet to decide on the type of day it would be.

"It was a nice change," Mariah said. "Mr. Carter always chooses depressing modern things. So dreary."

"Uh, right," Ellery said. "Mrs. Robertson, could I talk to you for a few minutes?"

"Of course!" She didn't seem at all surprised at his request, opening the door and backing up so Ellery could step inside the little cottage.

She led the way to a mercilessly tidy living room. Despite the abundance of accent pillows and doggie knickknacks, there was not a single speck of dust on a single surface. Nor did there seem to be any real-life doggies. The TV was on and tuned to the Hallmark Channel, which, despite the fact that it was June, seemed to be showing a Christmas movie.

"Please sit down. Would you like a cup of coffee?" Mariah said.

"That would be nice."

Mariah vanished into another room, and Ellery studied the rows and rows of framed photos covering the walls. It was unexpectedly disheartening to see the Robertson family dwindle from a stocky, grinning, confident trio to a strained and graying duo, to... No more photos. The last photo had probably been taken ten years ago.

But it was easy to follow the trajectory of Steve's life from grinning, gap-toothed kindergartener to scowling high-school quarterback. There were photos of Steve on fishing trips and escorting girls to proms—never the same girl twice—and holding aloft a variety of trophies and gold cups.

"That's my son, Stevie," Mariah said from behind Ellery. How could a woman holding a tray of china cups and cookies move so quietly?

"I know," Ellery said. "I was hoping I could talk to you about Steve."

She smiled that wide, hazy smile. "Of course. I always love to talk about Stevie."

Ellery rearranged some accent pillows and found space to sit on the sofa across from Mariah. They went through the business of cream and sugar, one cookie or two, and Ellery realized that what seemed so easy and even natural in mystery novels—questioning strangers about private matters—was actually kind of a huge intrusion. He couldn't help a cowardly wish that he'd let Nora and Mrs. Nelson do the interviewing after all.

"Stevie was a wonderful son," Mariah said, while Ellery was still trying to think of an inoffensive opening. "He was a wonderful boy, and he would have been a wonderful man. Like his father." She smiled at the gray-faced, gray-haired older version of Steve in the final photo on the opposite wall.

"He didn't want to attend college with his friends?" Ellery asked. It was the most innocuous thing he could think of as an icebreaker.

"He could have gone. He got all kinds of sports scholarships offered to him. He didn't want that. His friends weren't going to college, and he was needed here."

"Sure," Ellery said.

"He'd already learned everything school could teach him."

"Of course."

Mariah said, "The plan was always that he'd go into the business with his father."

"The business?"

She said proudly, "Robertson's Garage."

That did sort of ring a bell. Robertson's was the only garage on the island. With so much of Pirate's Cove closed off to automobile traffic, a lot of islanders didn't even own cars, preferring golf carts and bicycles. Ellery said, "So that worked out nicely."

"Yes."

"Did Steve ever have any...problems with anyone?"

She looked blank. "Problems?"

"Like run-ins with people?"

"Only on the football field."

So much for leading the witness.

"Did Steve have a girlfriend?"

"No." Maybe she thought that didn't reflect well on Steve because she corrected, "Girls were always pestering him, making fools of themselves, calling him all hours of the day and night." She shook her head in scorn. "Tramps. He didn't take any of them seriously. He was waiting for the right girl to come along."

Ellery said cautiously, "What about Rebecca Witherspoon? Did they date?"

The change in Mariah was instantaneous. She paled—which was saying something, since she already looked like a ghost—and then two bright-red spots appeared in her cheeks. Her colorless eyes blazed with emotion. "*Never.*"

"I'm sorry." Ellery wasn't exactly sure what he was apologizing for.

"That *bitch.*" Mariah's eyes welled with sudden tears. "Steve never wanted anything to do with her. She was like all the others; she was just stuck on herself." Her face twisted. "Acting like she was something special, too good for anyone else. And then pretending Stevie was chasing *her*, pestering *her.*"

"I really don't know much about it," Ellery said, which was certainly true.

"And then her friends claiming Stevie was to blame for what happened, that he brought it on himself. Terrible lies. How could people say such things?"

"People like to talk." Ellery was in a position to know.

"Yes, even when they don't know what they're talking about!" Mariah wiped her tears.

"But no one really knows what happened the night your son died, right?" Ellery asked. "There were no witnesses. No one admitted going to Skull House."

Her face distorted itself again. "No one admitted it, but there wasn't any secret who was there. Those kids ran in a pack."

"A pack…"

"Like wolves," Mariah said.

"When you say it wasn't a secret who was there, do you mean you know who some of those people were?"

She said darkly, "I've got a pretty good guess."

"Could you s—"

"Afterward everyone was so sorry about Becky Witherspoon." She mimicked, "*She was such a good student! Such nice manners! So pretty!* She *couldn't* be to blame. Not her. All that sympathy for *her*, and she was the one who started it! What about Stevie? What about my boy?"

Why had he imagined that the years would have dulled this woman's grief and anger? This was the kind of loss that no amount of time healed. Mariah was still as raw as slaughtered beef. And as intense as her grief was, her anger was even more ferocious.

"I'm sorry," Ellery said, and this time he was, this time he had an inkling of what he'd done in opening this shadow box of memories. "I'm sure it's worse not ever knowing what really happened."

"I know exactly what happened. She lured him up there, fed him drinks and drugs, and killed him."

Having once been a teenaged boy, Ellery knew it didn't take much in the way of luring to get a kid to a party at a haunted house. Or to get a kid to sample whatever was circulating in the way of drugs and alcohol. But maybe Steve had been more pliable, more suggestible than his pugnacious photos indicated.

"And then killed herself?" Ellery offered.

Mariah gave a laugh that made the hair on the back of his neck stand up. "Becky Witherspoon never killed herself. Not that one. She thought too much of herself for that. Her friends spread that story to cover for her."

"Really? What do you think happened to her?"

"I think her parents smuggled her off the island. I think she sailed off and lived the life she always wanted to live. No remorse. No regrets. She was cold to the bone that one. She fooled everyone else, but she *never* fooled me."

"Did you ever hear a rumor that Rebecca moved back to the island?"

Mariah stared at him. "She wouldn't do that."

"No? Why?"

Her mouth twitched into a truly terrifying smile. She said softly, "Because I'd kill her."

The phone rang.

Mariah didn't blink. She continued to sit there smiling that scary smile at Ellery.

The phone kept ringing.

"Do you need to get that?" Ellery asked.

"No. There's no one left I want to talk to."

Ellery put his coffee cup and plate on the table. He rose. "Well, I've taken up enough of your time."

"All I have is time." Mariah cocked her head, studying him as though a thought had just occurred to her. "You never said why you wanted to know about Stevie."

"Oh. A friend of mine—Brandon Abbott?—was hoping to write about the case—"

She went rigid. "*Him?*"

He'd read about "eyes starting from someone's head," but this was the first time he'd ever seen it. Mariah's pale eyes protruded with horror.

"Is there a problem?" Ellery asked.

"There is if you're here on *his* behalf!"

"No. No, I just hadn't heard about it...about the murder before, and I..." *Really?* Was she really supposed to believe that stumbling non-answer? Why hadn't he come prepared with a decent cover story? The problem was Nora and Mrs. Nelson had rushed him into this interview. Maybe he *should* have let them handle it.

"I want you to get out of my house," Mariah said, and her voice wobbled as though she was about to cry.

Oh no. Oh God.

"I'm sorry. Yes. I'm going," Ellery said quickly. "I didn't mean to upset you."

"*Get out!*" She jumped to her feet and came charging toward him.

For a second, astonishment held him motionless. She was *tiny*. He was six feet tall. What did she think she was going to do to him? Bite his ankles? But the look on her face was genuinely frightening.

Ellery turned and fled.

As he went out the front door, Mariah slammed it after him with such force, the head of the seagull door knocker fell to the steps and bounced into the overgrown grass.

CHAPTER TWELVE

Mrs. Nelson was not at the Crow's Nest when Ellery returned after interviewing Mariah Robertson. That was the good news. The bad news was, neither were any customers.

Nora was busily dusting the row of ship lanterns lining the back wall. She looked up hopefully at the jangle of the front door bell and came to meet him.

"Oh, it's you, dearie. How did it go?"

"I'm pretty sure I didn't learn anything we didn't already know. Well, except Brandon went to see Mariah."

"Did he now!"

"Which makes sense. She's an obvious person to talk to for someone writing a book about Skull House. But here's the thing, she came unglued when I said I was a friend of Brandon's." Ellery considered Mariah's reaction. "She didn't mind talking to me about the case, so I'm not sure why."

Nora said dryly, "Perhaps she's familiar with his work."

"Ha."

"It isn't as though he would have handled the tragedy with any sensitivity or taste."

True. Brandon's literary fortunes had not been built on his sensitivity or taste.

Ellery said, "She hates Rebecca and blames her for everything that happened. I guess that's understandable."

"Mariah was always blind to Steve's faults. The truth of the matter is Steve was a handsome dolt. I don't suppose he meant any harm by pestering Becky with his attentions—he probably believed he was flattering her—but nowadays we call it sexual harassment."

"Did Rebecca feel harassed?"

Nora hesitated. Admitted reluctantly, "I don't know. He irritated her, got under her skin, but that isn't always dislike. Perhaps on some level she was... unwillingly flattered."

"Mariah thinks Rebecca's parents got her off the island after Steve was killed."

Nora was silent. "That rumor circulated for a long time. Still circulates, I guess. I never saw two people more grief stricken. That's all I can say."

"More grief stricken than Mariah?" After all, even if Rebecca's parents had spirited her off the island, there would have been cause for grief.

"Well, no," Nora conceded. "Mariah went half-crazy. She's never been the same since."

They were silent for a moment.

"Anyway," Ellery began.

Nora said, "Were you able to get information about who went to the party that night?"

"No," Ellery said. "I didn't really have a chance. But she said it wasn't any secret."

"Yet she didn't offer any names? Didn't accuse anyone?"

"No."

"Did you ask her who Steve was dating at the time?"

"Uh…she did say he wasn't serious about any-one."

Nora waved that off. "He was serious about Becky. We already know that. But was there someone serious about *him*?"

"She said he always had a lot of girls pestering him."

"*Exactly.*"

"She probably doesn't know whether Steve dated or not. She doesn't just have an idealized memory; she thinks he was a candidate for sainthood."

"He was no saint."

"What kid his age is?" Ellery pointed out in the interest of fairness.

Nora let that go. "Did you ask her what she was doing the night Abbott died?"

Ellery stared. "*Her?* You think Mariah Robert-son could have killed Brandon?"

"You said she came unglued when you mentioned him."

"Well, sure, but…"

Nora shrugged. "We've yet to learn the modus operandi of this crime, but never underestimate the power of a woman."

"Right, but…"

"Someone killed him. That's certain."

"Is it?" Ellery said a little bitterly.

"We don't know yet what the police discovered, but we have to assume Chief Carson has justification to pursue this as a homicide investigation."

"Yeah, well," Ellery said. He glanced around the empty shop. "I think I'm going to head home. I left Watson crated. He's going to be barking down the house."

"Are you coming to the theater tonight?"

Ellery sighed. "I'd planned on it, but now I don't think so. I need a break. I may as well finish painting the entry hall at Captain's Seat before they throw me in jail."

Nora said briskly, "Now, now. Chief Carson won't let that happen."

"Sure about that?"

Nora studied his face. "Pretty sure."

Ellery smiled without humor. "We'll see. Detective Lansing seems to think he has the case all sewn up."

Nora said slowly, "Does he?"

"That was the impression I got. I'm surprised they let me walk out of there." He still felt sick when he remembered the shock of hearing he was Brandon's beneficiary, sick when he remembered Jack had let him walk into that interview completely unprepared, unsuspecting.

Nora looked thoughtful. "I wonder…"

She had such an odd expression. Ellery said, "What?"

"Nothing." Nora was frowning. "Just a funny idea. George Lansing is Mariah Robertson's nephew."

* * * * *

Ellery could hear Watson barking from outside the house.

He let himself inside, went to liberate the prisoner, and stoically accepted his punishment as Watson crawled all over him whining, yipping, and biting his nose.

"Oww," Ellery protested, returning the nips and licks with little kisses. "I'm sorry, but it's not like I had a choice."

There's always a choice, Watson returned, though not in so many words.

And that was the truth, wasn't it?

Jack had had a choice. A couple of choices. As much as Ellery wanted to be fair, it was hard to keep an open mind about a friend who seemed to believe you were capable of murder.

He took Watson outside and let him play around in the sunshine and fresh air, and then he began emptying out the long entry hall of furniture and artwork, carrying everything out into the overgrown front yard.

He was going to need an extension ladder to reach the top of the walls. Or maybe he could dangle over the staircase railings in a climbing harness. Or maybe he should just break down and hire someone to do that part of the painting.

Or maybe it was all moot because he'd be sitting in prison for the next twenty years for a crime he didn't commit.

After he had emptied the hall, he set about taping the baseboards and wooden trim of the curving staircase. That took a while because first he had to clean several years of dust and grime from the molding before the tape would stick.

Once he had untangled Watson for the third time and the tape was in place, Ellery spread out his tarp, opened the first can of silvery-blue "Moonmist," and began to paint.

There was something unexpectedly soothing about the work, the relief of uncomplicated physical exertion, yes, and also the satisfaction brought by slow, steady sweeps of the roller covering the smudged, gray walls, transforming the room with every spinning glide of paint.

The misty blue worked even better than he had anticipated, reflecting the sunlight streaming from the porthole window high above and transforming the space. Somehow the contrast of cool color served to warm the dark planks of the floor and railing so that the entire hall seemed to glow, as bright and airy as the breeze from the sea.

Ellery worked steadily from the end of the hall toward the front door without stopping for lunch or any real break. The light began to fade. By then his muscles were starting to shake and his stomach was growling. He had been too angry and heartsick to even think of food before, but now he was starving, and he began to give some thought to what he had in the fridge.

Knock. Knock. Knock.

The hard rap of knuckles on the front door frame jolted him out of his preoccupation, caused him to overbalance. The ladder tipped one way; Ellery tipped the other. He let out a yowl as he fell sideways.

He managed to grab the top of the door, and then hard arms locked around his waist.

He landed lightly, still off balance though this time it had nothing to do with falling and everything to do with being in another man's arms—the confusing rush of a lean body pressing against his, warm breath against his face, the gleam of bright sea-colored eyes gazing into his own—however briefly.

Jack.

The funny thing was he'd known it was Jack before he ever saw his face. Maybe he'd subconsciously registered his aftershave or his shoes.

Ellery pulled free and stepped back. "What are you doing here?"

"Whoa," Jack said, which could have referred to Ellery's hostile tone or Ellery's near collision with the timber flooring. Jack put his hands up in a Don't Kill the Messenger gesture. "I came to make sure you're all right."

"You're playing good cop now?"

Jack's face tightened. "Okay, that's not fair."

"You know what's not fair? What you did to me this morning."

Jack looked momentarily discomfited but recovered fast. "Look. I didn't enjoy that, but I have a job to do. And that job requires that I maintain an open mind regarding this investigation. There's a reason I'm not taking lead on this case. That reason is you."

"Believe me, I get it."

"Do you? Because you seem to be blaming me for something I have no control over."

"Give me a blankety-blanking break," Ellery said—although, in fact, he did not say *blankety-blanking*.

"Feel free to tell me how you think you'd have handled it," Jack said.

"I don't know. I'm not a cop. I think I'd have said something like, *Hey, Ellery, you need to come down here and answer some questions for me and Detective Lansing, who's running this investigation.* I think I'd have tried not to blindside a friend. But blindsiding me was the point, wasn't it?"

Jack didn't bother to deny it. "So far, the little evidence we have points to you. People would ask questions—rightfully so—if you hadn't been brought in for questioning."

"Except I wasn't brought in for questioning— not a routine questioning, anyway. Detective Lansing's already convinced I'm guilty. He clearly thinks he's got this whole case wrapped up."

"Well, he's wrong." Jack looked and sounded tired, but Ellery refused to soften. He was tired too. And worried.

"Is he? Are you so sure? Or do you maybe deep-down kind of wonder if I *did* kill Brandon?"

For one split-second, Jack hesitated.

That was it as far as Ellery was concerned. He said bleakly, "That's what I thought. Go away, Jack. You did your duty. I'm fine. You're the last person I want to talk to now."

He turned away and picked the fallen paint roller off the tarp, deliberately ignoring Jack, who stood motionless, not speaking, just watching him.

After a moment or two, Jack turned without a word and went outside. Still bent over, Ellery spared a quick glance for the rigid shoulders and ramrod straight line of Jack's back as he retreated down the steps and crossed the white gravel to his service vehicle.

So much for the start of a beautiful friendship.

Ellery had won that battle, but it didn't give him any pleasure. He felt sad and discouraged and, unreasonably, a smidge guilty. What sense did that make? Why should he feel guilty? Jack was the one in the wrong. Wasn't he?

Watson, who had watched the entire exchange with clear puzzlement that his leaps and whines for attention had gone unnoticed, glanced at Ellery and started to follow Jack outside.

"No, Watson," Ellery ordered.

Was it possible to see a puppy's face fall? Watson had an almost human look of disappointment on his little puss.

Ellery gathered up the paint tray, brushes, and roller, kicked the front door shut, and carried everything into the kitchen, dropping his load in the huge farmhouse-style sink. He turned on the taps full blast, braced his arms on the sink, and hung his head.

You know it's a bad day when the only bright spot is you haven't been arrested yet.

He opened his eyes, watching the watery swirl of pale blue circle and vanish, gurgling, down the drain.

"I don't think you killed Brandon," Jack said gruffly from behind him.

The rush of water had drowned his approach. Ellery's head snapped up so fast, he nearly threw his back out, and he whirled around.

Jack was holding Watson, who gazed adoringly up at him. "He was out in the front yard." Jack handed the puppy over like a peace offering.

Ellery took Watson. The puppy tried to lick his chin.

"Thanks," Ellery said stiffly. "I must not have closed the door properly." He kissed Watson's silky head, not meeting Jack's eyes.

Jack said, "I *don't* think you murdered Brandon. I don't think you're capable of murder. Not calculated, cold-blooded murder. But I'm a cop. I worked homicide for more years than I want to remember. And one of the first lessons I learned was—"

"Good people do bad things," Ellery finished. "You told me that before."

"Did I? Well, it's true. You're the only person on this island with any kind of a relationship to our victim. You fought with him the day he died."

"We had an argument. Yes. It ended with us still planning to meet for drinks. I've had arguments with you too, Jack. Are you in fear of your life?"

Jack didn't bother to answer that. "You went to his house that very night. You 'found' a threatening note I didn't see when I walked through a few minutes earlier—"

Ellery gasped. "Are you accusing me of—"

"Will you let me finish? You're the sole beneficiary of Abbott's estate. There's a mountain of circumstantial but damning evidence against you."

"Which is why it would be…nice…to have the support of my friends." To Ellery's chagrin, his voice wavered a little on the word *friends*. "At the least, you could have encouraged me to hire a lawyer."

Jack shook his head. "You're not looking at this clearly. If you'd lawyered up—at my suggestion, no less—it would've sent a message to the team that even *I* think you're guilty. If I tried to run interference for you, you'd look *more* guilty. I'd be accused of bias, and even after you're exonerated—and you will be in time, I have no doubt of that—some people would always think, and would certainly keep the whispers going, that you got off because I covered up for you."

People like Sue Lewis. Not that she bothered to whisper when she could use the *Scuttlebutt Weekly* as a megaphone.

This was an angle Ellery had not considered, and he wasn't sure what to think, let alone say.

"Look, being a cop makes you cynical. I don't deny it. And I'm sorry for that. But I *am* your friend," Jack said. "You do have my support, even if I can't show it the same way as Nora or Dylan or Sandy. That's all. That's what I came back to say."

Ellery's throat had closed. Too tight to say anything without spilling everything. He had to settle for a curt nod.

Maybe Jack was expecting more, but Ellery was still hurt, still feeling betrayed by the memory of that interview in Jack's office—and also by the recollection that Jack had opted against pursuing a closer relationship.

"Okay. Well." Jack shoved his hands in the pockets of his Levi's. He nodded. "Have a good evening." He headed for the door.

Ellery managed to pry out a compressed, "Thanks, Jack."

Jack glanced back, gave him a funny smile. "You're welcome, Ellery."

He turned and disappeared through the doorway.

CHAPTER THIRTEEN

The Internet was in mourning.

By Monday morning Brandon's murder had hit all the major news outlets, and Brandon's fans were grieving loudly with gifs and memes posted all across the World Wide Web.

Happily, Ellery's name did not appear in any of the initial reports of Brandon's death. That would change once the Associated Press picked up Sue Lewis's "articles" for the *Scuttlebutt Weekly*, which was bound to happen however much Ellery prayed otherwise. Pirate's Cove would be lucky if big-city reporters didn't show up on their shores. Brandon's passing was even bigger news than Ellery had anticipated.

Partly, of course, because it was murder. Murder was always news.

PCPD Detective George Lansing revealed that while the police have identified a person of interest in the case, they had not yet exhausted all other avenues of investigation.

"Terrific," Ellery muttered.

He wasted an unbelievable amount of time googling—and goggling over—twitter threads and message boards lamenting the loss of Brandon's influence and genius.

Influence? Sure. Brandon had been a bestselling author of commercial fiction. He sold millions of books and had movies regularly produced from his work—some of which Ellery preferred not to remember. But a *genius*? Come on!

He did learn that Brandon had been sued successfully over *House Full of Ghosts*, which was inspired by a grisly murder in Kansas. Unfortunately for Brandon, this real-life cold case involved some still very much alive participants who had not taken kindly to having their kinfolk accused of both homicide and demonic possession. The lawsuit had cost Brandon a pretty penny. Worse, one of the plaintiffs had made several physical threats against Brandon.

Granted, Kansas was a long way from Rhode Island, and both the lawsuit and threats were three years old. Still, here was a potential lead. Here was a potential suspect. Would anyone at PCPD bother to check it out? Doubtful. Not when Detective Lansing was so sure he had his case tied up with a bow.

If PCPD hadn't managed to catch Steve Robertson's killer twenty years ago, how likely were they to solve this one?

In fairness, Lansing would probably have been about ten years old at the time of his cousin's murder. But Jack had tried to tackle the cold case when he'd first moved to Pirate's Cove, and he hadn't any luck. If Jack couldn't solve it, what chance did Lansing have?

Ellery listened to his thoughts and winced.

Did he really think that much of Jack?

Well, yeah. Kind of.

Anyway.

Business was slow. Then again, it was always slow during the week. It was not *quite* as slow as it had been when he was suspected of killing Trevor. So that was a good sign. Maybe some of his fellow villagers were going to give him the benefit of the doubt this time.

Shortly before lunch, Aunt Eudora's lawyer returned his phone call.

Mr. Landry regretted that he did not have experience in trying criminal cases, but assured Ellery he could recommend someone experienced if it came to that. He felt confident it *wouldn't* come to that.

"I'm not so sure," Ellery said.

"No Page has ever been convicted of murder," Mr. Landry informed him.

Which started Ellery wondering what those previous Pages *had* been convicted of. And whether the lack of convictions was more about a good legal defense than actual innocence.

Shortly *after* lunch he got another call from a lawyer. Mr. Honeycutt had represented Brandon in life and in death, and was phoning to let Ellery know he was Brandon's sole beneficiary. Detective Lansing had already broken this news to Ellery, so it wasn't the shock it would have once been.

"I don't know what to say," Ellery said truthfully.

Mr. Honeycutt discussed the logistics of online conferencing and DocuSign, and then admitted, "It's not quite the windfall it would have been five years ago. The lawsuit was very costly. And, sadly, Mr. Abbott's books have not performed as well as they once did. In fact, his last three titles have yet to earn out their advances."

"He was broke?" Ellery asked.

Mr. Honeycutt hemmed and hawed, but yes, that was pretty much the gist of it. Definitely, Brandon had been cash poor. Honeycutt offered the helpful observation that now that Brandon was dead, his book sales were likely to skyrocket. Naturally, being a lawyer, Honeycutt phrased it more diplomatically, but his point seemed to be that Brandon was definitely worth more dead than alive.

"So *that's* why he decided to move into Skull House?" Ellery deduced.

"The other properties have all been sold or mortgaged to the hilt," Mr. Honeycutt agreed. "Mr. Abbott was able to purchase the Buck Island property outright, and in time it should prove a valuable investment. He pinned a great deal of hope on the success of his next book."

So much for that.

The bottom line was Brandon had bequeathed Ellery a strong motive for murder—and not much more.

Shortly after Ellery ended his call with Mr. Honeycutt, the mayor walked through the front door of the Crow's Nest, looking as pained and uncomfortable as a baby with gas.

"Ellery, my boy, could I have a word in private?" He cast a meaningful look Nora's way.

Nora sniffed loudly and returned to her filing.

"Sure," Ellery said, leading the way to his office. He wasn't sure what this was about, but he had a feeling it wasn't going to be pleasant.

Cyrus paced up and down in front of Ellery's desk, seemingly too nervous to sit. Ellery closed the door to his office.

"What's up, Cyrus?"

Cyrus cleared his throat. "Ellery, you and I have always had a friendly relationship, so I hope you won't take this the wrong way. Mariah Robertson has filed a complaint with the city council."

"She..." He had to admit, he hadn't seen that coming. "I see."

"She's accused you of harassing her in her own home."

Would it have been preferable to harass her outside her home? Ellery wondered. He didn't say it, of course. He could see Cyrus studying him, that his brown gaze was curious—and worried.

"Harassing her? That's pretty strong. I stopped by to ask her some questions about Steve and Rebecca—"

"*Why?*" Cyrus broke in. "Why would you do that? You must've realized how insensitive, how hurtful those questions would be."

"To be honest, I didn't. I should have. I realize that now. But I was thinking so much time had passed—"

"Not for Steve's mother!"

"No. You're right."

"I just can't understand why you'd do such a thing. What did you hope to achieve?"

"Cyrus, there's a murderer loose in Pirate's Cove, and it's not me."

"Well, of course it's not you!" Cyrus said. "You're not taking Sue Lewis's editorials to heart, surely? Not again!"

"It's not just Sue Lewis who thinks I'm guilty. The police think I'm guilty."

Cyrus made a spluttery *Oh, nonsense!* sound.

"But they do," Ellery said. "Detective Lansing for sure does."

"Lansing can't do anything without Chief Carson's approval, and Carson—" Cyrus seemed to think better of whatever he had been about to say, substituting, "The chief is a fair man. He's not going to let anyone be railroaded."

"Sure, but so far I'm the only suspect, and there's a lot of circumstantial evidence against me. I can't just sit here twiddling my thumbs."

"No, but you could concentrate on running your business, which is what the city council expects of vendors."

Ouch. That was unexpectedly sharp coming from the kindly mayor. Maybe Cyrus recognized it, because he sighed. "You might not think it to look at her, but Mariah Robertson still holds a lot of sway with the council members. Antagonizing her is not a wise thing to do."

"I won't talk to her again."

Cyrus nodded. "I'm still unclear why you talked to her at *all*."

"I think it's too much of a coincidence that Brandon started poking around, asking questions about Steve Robertson's murder, and then he too suddenly ends up murdered."

Cyrus frowned. "You can't seriously think these deaths are connected!"

"You don't think that's a huge coincidence?"

"No! Of course not. We all know who killed young Steve. Besides, I don't think Abbott *was* murdered. I believe it was an accident."

"An accident? The police—"

Cyrus brushed that off. "The police have been wrong before. I'm sure the coroner's report will bear out what I'm saying. That Abbott's death was accidental."

Ellery couldn't help wondering if Cyrus had some pull with the coroner's office. He sounded so sure. More likely it was wishful thinking on his part.

"But if it *was* murder, that killer is still loose in Pirate's Cove," Ellery pointed out.

"If it was murder—and as I said, I don't believe it was—it'll turn out to be someone from Abbott's past. Such a strange, unsavory personality. You'll see. It's impossible that we would have a murderer running around Pirate's Cove."

Actually, not so much. They'd had a murderer running around Pirate's Cove only a few weeks earlier. But it seemed tactless to point that out, and in any case, Cyrus didn't wait for Ellery's reply.

"Please. For your own sake, my boy, for the sake of the village, don't stir up any more bad memories. No good can come from tearing open old wounds."

"I'm sorry I caused Mrs. Robertson any pain," Ellery said. He couldn't agree to what Cyrus was asking. Although he understood where Cyrus was coming from.

Cyrus, however, seemed to take his answer for a promise, because he looked relieved. "Good, good. I'm sorry if I seemed a little harsh. On the bright side, we had another wonderful performance last night. It's a shame you missed it."

Ellery smiled politely. He was glad Cyrus believed in his innocence, glad the play was doing well, but whether Cyrus realized it or not, being suspected of murder was highly stressful. The dramatic success of *Murder Mansion* was the last thing on Ellery's mind at the moment.

No, he needed to pursue his own investigation because he couldn't rely on the police to get it right. Even if the case fizzled out for lack of evidence, it would not be a relief. The shadow of suspicion would hang over him forever. Jack had been right about that.

Besides, maybe Brandon *had* been strange and occasionally unsavory, but he didn't deserve to be murdered.

Cyrus's visit made one thing clear: Ellery needed to be a lot more discreet in his sleuthing.

He opened the office door and saw Cyrus out, still smiling and nodding as Cyrus talked about the play and, of course, how brilliant Felix was in it.

"He's a very talented kid," Ellery agreed.

"Thank you for understanding, my boy," Cyrus told Ellery, patting his back. He waved a cheery goodbye to Nora who—still offended at the implication she couldn't keep her mouth shut—pretended not to see, and took himself off.

The bookshop door swung closed with a cheery chime, and Ellery returned to the front counter.

"I hope you didn't listen to him," Nora said.

"I hope *you* didn't listen to him," Ellery retorted.

Nora tossed her head. "I don't need to eavesdrop to guess why the Honorable Cyrus Jones showed up on our doorstep this afternoon."

"That makes one of us. I knew Mrs. Robertson was upset yesterday, but I really didn't expect her to go to the town fathers."

"I suppose we should have anticipated it. Mariah has a…a veritable mania about Steve. But there was no way around it. We needed to hear what she had to say."

"I'm not sure it was worth having my business license yanked."

Nora looked shocked. "Cyrus never threatened you with putting us out of business?"

"It was more tactful than that. But I got the message loud and clear. Poking into the past is not encouraged."

Nora made a dismissive noise.

Ellery said, "It's always possible Brandon's death *isn't* tied to the history of Skull House. He made his share of enemies over the years."

"Possible but not probable," Nora said. "Now, I've been thinking who you could talk to next. My niece Nan was good friends with Becky."

"Nan!" Ellery eyed her suspiciously. "Wait a minute. You're not sending me out on wild goose chase interviews just to keep me busy, are you?"

"Certainly not." Nora seemed genuinely surprised. "We don't have time to waste on that kind of foolishness. Regardless of what Cyrus imagines, you're in real danger of being arrested for this murder. We need to gather enough information to redirect the police investigation, and we need to do it quickly."

Ellery's stomach knotted. On the whole, he tended to believe Nora over Cyrus, as much as he wished Cyrus's version of current events to be true.

Nora was saying, "Nan might very well have some insights into what happened that night at Skull House."

"Was Nan there that night?"

"She's always denied it," Nora said. "I've always believed she was lying."

"Nice."

"Not one teenager on this island ever admitted going to Skull House that night, or any other time," Nora said. "I think it's safe to assume at least some of them are lying."

"You sound as cynical as Jack Carson."

"All historians are cynics. If the past teaches us anything, it's to be suspicious."

Ellery laughed.

Nora said, "If Becky did run away that night, she might have told Nan where she was going."

"But would Nan have kept something like that to herself? I mean, another kid *died*."

"Nan's very loyal. If she believed Becky was defending herself or that there were extenuating circumstances, she might have tried to protect her. Even if it did mean lying to the police. Our chief back then was...well, he was no Jack Carson, let's leave it at that. He didn't have much patience for teenagers and the feeling went both ways."

An idea occurred to Ellery. "Teenagers... If we're correct and Brandon's murder *is* tied to Steve's, then we're looking at a relatively small age group of potential suspects. Late thirties to early forties, right?"

"Excellent observation! We'll make a detective of you yet."

Ellery grinned. "That's what I'm afraid of."

Nora was busy doing some mental calculations. "I think the youngest attendee would likely have been Janet Maples. She'd have been about seventeen."

"Janet? I thought she was in her fifties."

"No. Though I imagine life with Trevor added a few years to her mind and body." Nora half closed her eyes, considering. "I suspect the eldest would have been Sandy Morita."

"Our Sandy? Sandy next door?" Not that there could be two Sandy Moritas in a village the size of Pirate's Cove.

"That's right. She was a little older, a sophomore in college, but she was friends with Becky and Nan."

"Would George Lansing have been there?" Ellery asked on impulse.

"Detective Lansing? He'd have been a little boy. I can't imagine..." Nora had a funny expression on her face. "He did worship the ground Steve walked on. I suppose there's a slim chance he followed him that night, but if he'd seen anything useful, he'd surely have spoken up."

"True. I can't think of a good reason he wouldn't." Then again, he couldn't think of a good reason any of the kids there that night wouldn't have spoken up. Oh, maybe not at the time, but twenty years later? If they were still keeping quiet, surely it was because they didn't have anything to tell?

Or was he looking at that backward?

Were they all keeping quiet because they *did* know something? Something that still scared them twenty years later?

CHAPTER FOURTEEN

Unfortunately, Ellery's plan to casually drop by the Seacrest Inn that afternoon and interview Nan Sweeny was derailed by an unexpected visit from Police Chief Carson.

And it was definitely Police Chief Carson, not Jack, glowering at Ellery from the front entrance. Even the bell swaying on the door had a *It Tolls For Thee* kind of ring to it.

"We. Need. To. Talk." Jack's tone was as uncompromising as his expression.

At least this time Ellery was prepared. He'd guessed that if Mayor Jones felt it necessary to come calling, Jack would not be far behind. So he was braced for this, but it was still kind of aggravating the way his heart jumped around in his chest as though the sight of Jack on the horizon was always good news.

This was definitely not going to be good news.

"I-I'll just go grab a coffee," Nora said hastily, scooting around Jack and darting out the door.

The bell tolled again.

Ellery beckoned toward his office. "Step into my lair."

"If you think this is funny—"

"I don't think it's funny. I make jokes when I'm nervous. You know that."

Jack's eyes narrowed, but he didn't disagree. "What in God's name did you think you were doing going to see Mariah Robertson?"

"I don't understand what the outrage is over me going to ask that woman a couple of questions."

Jack snapped out, "The *outrage* is at you harassing a—"

"I didn't harass her! She fed me coffee and cookies, so how harassed could she have felt?"

He saw that information register with Jack. He was quieter, though still terse, as he replied, "Harassed enough to go to the police afterward."

"The police *and* the town council? You know, I'm finding her behavior very suspicious."

Jack gave a disbelieving laugh. "*Her* behavior?"

"Yes! She didn't have a single objection to a single question I asked until I mentioned being friends with Brandon. Then she blew up. What does that tell you?"

Jack said, "That she was trying to be polite until she learned you were a friend of the man who planned on sensationalizing and trivializing her only child's death."

"She wasn't being polite. She *wanted* to talk about Steve. And I *wasn't* harassing her. I asked her a few simple questions, that's all. And when I saw she was upset, I apologized and left. I didn't realize she was—that it was still so—"

"That isn't something you get over." The look on Jack's face, the darkness in his eyes, turned Ellery's heart cold. He understood this wasn't academic for Jack. That Jack had suffered that kind of tragedy. He had known Jack had lost his wife. Now he understood that there had been another loss, maybe the most painful loss of all.

It closed his throat like a vise. His words came out stifled and small. "It wasn't real to me until then," Ellery tried to explain. "It was just…another legend. Like Ann Rathbone and John Mansfield. I wasn't trying to cause her pain. I'm trying to—"

"I *know* what you're trying to do," Jack cut him off. "The entire village probably now knows what you're trying to do. This isn't the way. You need to leave this to me, to the police."

"I can't! I'm not going to prison for something I didn't do."

"I told you yesterday—"

"I don't care what you told me yesterday," Ellery cried. "Today there was another editorial from Sue Lewis all but accusing me of murdering Brandon. She's ruining me! Look around you, Jack. No one is coming into the Crow's Nest. Everyone thinks I did it. And your Detective Lansing isn't even going to consider whether Brandon's death is tied to the past because he's not going to want his cousin's murder dredged up again."

"Okay, wait a minute. Stop," Jack ordered in a different voice.

Ellery stopped.

"We've had this conversation before, and not that long ago. You are *not* an officer of the law. You sell books. You make movies. You write plays. You do not, do *not* solve crimes."

"I've done it before."

"The hell," Jack returned. Loudly. "We both know you stumbled over the solution last time. That was a lucky guess. You almost ended up dead."

True. All of it. Which, as far as Ellery was concerned, changed nothing.

He said flatly, "I'm not sitting here and letting someone frame me for murder. Sorry."

"*Sorry?*" Jack actually paled. "I'm not *requesting* that you stay out of this case, Ellery. I'm *ordering* you to stay out of it. Do you hear me?"

"I hear you."

Jack's eyes narrowed. "Do you understand?"

"Yep. I understand."

Jack stared at him. His mouth twisted into a hard smile. "But you don't agree? Okay. You've said you didn't kill Abbott, and I believe you, which means Abbott's killer is still out there. What do you think will happen when he—or she—figures out what you're up to?"

Unease slithered down Ellery's spine. He had been wondering the same thing ever since his conversation with the mayor. Mostly he was hoping his efforts would go undetected. He said lightly, "Maybe they're long gone. Brandon made a few enemies over the years. Maybe whoever killed him doesn't even live on the island. Maybe they left on the next morning's ferry."

"Maybe. But if you really believed that, you wouldn't have interviewed Mariah Robertson." Jack gave another of those steely smiles. "It isn't hard to follow your line of reasoning. It certainly won't be hard for the person you're hunting."

He couldn't really argue with that, so he said nothing.

Jack regarded him. Finally, he said more quietly, "I'm not saying this to you because I'm afraid of the competition or because I'm afraid you'll mess our case up with your amateurish efforts. I'm telling you this because I'm worried. I'm concerned. I don't want anything to happen to you. Is that clear enough?"

Welllll… Yes and no. Ellery was unwillingly warmed by Jack's concern—and equal parts confused. For a straightforward kind of guy, Jack's messaging was consistently…mixed. Though not the part about butting out. *That* was plain enough.

"I appreciate your concern," Ellery said. "I promise I'll be as careful as I know how. If by some chance I do happen to discover anything, you know I'll come straight to you. It's just…I can't sit by, waiting to be arrested. Once was bad enough. I can't do it again. It's making me crazy."

Jack nodded, not in agreement, but acknowledging what Ellery was saying. "I'm holding you to that. If you come up with anything, I want to know."

"You'll be the first," Ellery promised. He sincerely hoped that was true, but he had the uncomfortable suspicion someone else, someone dangerous would probably know before either Jack or himself.

* * * * *

"Here's the man of the hour!" Dylan exclaimed when Ellery showed up at his house for Monday Night Scrabble.

Ellery stepped inside, sketching a general wave to Tom Tulley, Libby, Janet Maples, Sandy, Mr. Starling, and Greta Handel, owner of the gourmet grocery store on Mizzen Street, who were already crowded into Dylan's front room. He'd known from the cars and golf carts parked in the lane outside Dylan's cottage that he was the last to show up that evening.

"That's me," Ellery said. "They'll be giving me the keys to the city any day now."

"There's the spirit." Dylan squeezed his shoulder. More quietly, he said, "I'm glad you showed up, kiddo. Never let them see you sweat."

Ellery half grimaced, half smiled. He'd been tempted to cancel—he was not in the mood for games, not even his beloved Scrabble—but it had occurred to him that if he didn't show, he was liable to look guilty, plus, he needed all the friends he could get right now. Besides, what kind of amateur sleuth would miss the golden opportunity of hobnobbing with some of the best informed of Pirate's Cove's insiders.

"The city jail, perhaps," Janet Maples drawled from the long leather sofa. She was a tall, pencil-thin woman with long, stick-straight hair and round spectacles. She owned Old Salt Stationary.

"Now, Janet," Dylan chided, steering Ellery into the low-ceilinged, comfortable room lined with framed theatrical posters. "Be good."

"Glad to see you up and around again, Janet," Ellery said. What he was actually thinking was Janet still looked a little ghostly after her recent close call.

Janet groaned. "God. Don't be nice on top of everything else. It's humiliating enough owing my life to you."

Everyone laughed, and Ellery relaxed. He'd been a little uncertain of what kind of reception he'd receive from the Scrabblers now that he was once again the prime suspect in a murder investigation. It was almost a relief that Janet was back to her usual sardonic form.

Dylan asked, "What'll you have to drink?"

"A lot."

Everyone laughed again, indicating they were well ahead of him in that department.

"We're trying out Blueberry Icebergs," Libby called.

"Oh, are we?" her father said. Libby stuck her tongue out. "I'm nineteen, Pop. Don't nag."

Funny, until that moment it hadn't occurred to Ellery that both Felix and Libby were the age of the kids who attended that fateful and fatal party at Skull House. No wonder no one had shown any good judgment that night. *Oh.* That meant their parents were old enough to have been there when it all went down.

No. Wrong. Cyrus was at least fifty. Felix was the product of a second marriage. But Tom… Tom was definitely the right age. Ellery studied the owner of the Salty Dog with new interest.

Like his adored only child, Tom was tall and ginger-haired. He had the same twinkling blue eyes and ready laugh. Unlike his daughter, he had shoulders like a stevedore and a nose that had been broken several times over the years.

"Do you know Greta?" Dylan asked.

Ellery and Greta admitted they had never met, and introductions were made. Greta was probably in her forties, stocky and tanned with a silver pageboy. She volunteered that she had only lived on Buck Island for three years.

"How are you holding up, Ellery?" Dylan's gaze was intent and concerned.

It was a source of mutual amusement that when he'd first met Dylan, he'd assumed he was of the same orientation. It turned out Dylan was just a flamboyant guy with a slightly effeminate manner. In fact, Dylan was quite the ladies' man.

Ellery, conscious that they had an audience, could feel his smile turn lopsided. "I'm okay. I should be used to it by now, right?"

Dylan shook his head. "I used to think I knew Sue Lewis."

Mr. Starling, gazing as though hypnotized into the depths of his cobalt martini, called, "Don't you worry, son. Chief Carson will figure it out. He's a very smart man, our sheriff."

"He's police chief, Stan," Tom said.

"Tomato, tomahto." Mr. Starling waved his hand vaguely.

"I wouldn't hold my breath," Janet said. "He didn't figure it out the last time."

Ellery assumed Janet was referring to Trevor's murder, but Sandy said, "In fairness, it was a cold case by then."

Janet shrugged.

Ellery said, "Then you think Brandon's murder is connected to what happened twenty years ago?"

He could feel an almost instant change in the air, and could have kicked himself for speaking up. They were tipsy enough, or had forgotten for a moment, that this was not a closed circle of friends.

Janet said airily, "That's the legend, right? Skull House is cursed." She handed her empty glass to Libby, who headed for the wet bar in the corner of the front room.

"We should probably set the boards up if we're going to play tonight," Sandy said.

Ellery took a chance. "But no one really wants the truth of what happened at Skull House twenty years ago to come out, do they?"

There was an astonished silence.

"Why would you say that?" Sandy asked. She seemed genuinely shocked.

"Wouldn't the people who were there that night have spoken up?"

He couldn't believe it when Janet instinctively looked at Tom and Tom glanced at Sandy. They might as well have had *Invitation to Party* mimeographed across their foreheads. It couldn't have been more obvious. But then, as Mariah had pointed out, in Pirate's Cove, it probably really wasn't that much of a secret who had been there that night. The partiers would certainly have known, and their parents and employers would have had to have a pretty good guess. No, that seemingly impenetrable wall was for outsiders like himself—and law enforcement.

"No offense, Page, but you don't know what you're talking about," Tom said. He was smiling and easy, but there was a warning glint in his eyes.

"Wow," Libby said. "This sure turned dark fast."

Greta was wide-eyed, looking from one face to the next.

Janet said, "Anyway, I came here tonight to reclaim my title as Scrabble champion, not—"

"*Of course* we all want the truth," Sandy interrupted. "It's not that simple."

"Or constructive," Janet said.

Dylan, who had been quietly making drinks at the bar, brought Ellery a martini. His gaze, meeting Ellery's, seemed to urge caution.

"Sure. Let's play," Ellery said. "I didn't mean to ruin the mood."

"You didn't. It's ancient history," Janet said.

"Nah. It's forgotten," Tom said, which was surely wishful thinking on his part.

The scrabble boards were set up in the dining room and the group broken into two teams. Janet, Tom, Libby, and Sandy were on one team. Ellery, Dylan, Mr. Starling, and Greta on the other. It was a little quiet at first, perhaps a little awkward, as they began to play. As quiet as Ellery's team was, the team a few seats down the long dining table appeared to be conducted in a morgue.

"Who wants another drink?" Dylan asked after about ten minutes of taking turns to achieve such lame but legit results as ZYZZYVA and—hooking onto ZYZZYVA—ZAX, which had sparked Mr. Starling to resurrect what was clearly a long-standing debate about whether foreign words should be allowed.

"I do!" Ellery said, and everyone else piped up with relief.

Dylan sped to the living room with Libby to assist, and Greta said, "I feel like we should be holding a séance."

Another of those odd pauses followed.

"An eight-point word, for what it's worth," Janet said. "Maybe we should have tried that."

No one said a word. Greta looked at Ellery in inquiry. Mr. Starling pulled out a gray silk hanky and began polishing his diamond-bright spectacles.

Dylan and Libby returned with trays of midnight-blue cocktails, and playing resumed.

Ellery's turn came again. He added R, N, I, N, G to T and U. "TURNING, ten points."

"Hm." Dylan was unimpressed.

As though thinking aloud, Mr. Starling murmured, "Even if that writer fellow's murder is connected to what happened twenty years ago, it doesn't mean she—it doesn't mean he was killed by the same person."

"Of course he wasn't," Sandy said. "Of course these crimes weren't connected."

Her teammates stared at her.

"What? *Of course* they're connected," Janet said.

"But they can't be," Sandy protested.

"Don't be ridiculous." Janet sounded tired. "It defies belief that Abbott would start poking around, end up dead, and it's only a coincidence?"

"That's it." Tom stood up, slightly rocking the dining table. "I've had enough for one night. Libby, get your coat."

"*Pop—*"

"Get your coat," Tom ordered, and from Libby's expression, it was pretty clear that was not a tone of voice she often heard from her doting dad.

Libby jumped up, stalked from the room, and Ellery exchanged apologetic glances with Dylan. Never mind being a mood killer, he couldn't help feeling his presence had proved to be a catalyst that evening. He wasn't completely sorry, though; in fact, he was very much intrigued by the dynamics between Tom, Sandy, and Janet. At least he had an idea of who he could try interviewing next. Not that he would get far with Tom. Or Janet. But he and Sandy were friends. Maybe she would prove easier to crack. Er, talk to.

Greta, meanwhile, looked totally confused, and Mr. Starling was saying, "Did I say something? I'm sorry if I offended anyone."

"Nope, no problem," Tom said brusquely. "I've got an early start tomorrow."

"You run a pub," Janet said. "How early do your customers begin drinking?"

Tom threw his head back and yelled, "LIBBY!"

"Jeez. *Coming.*" Libby pulled on her blue teddy-bear coat as she hurried into the dining room. "I don't see what the big deal is. It's not like everyone in the village isn't talking about this. Even Felix's dad is fuming."

Tom ignored her, turning to Ellery. "Listen, Page, nobody thinks what Sue Lewis is trying to do to you is right. But poking your nose into the past isn't going to help you. It might just get you killed."

Janet and Sandy gasped, staring at Tom in horror. Libby's eyes were anime-sized.

"*Pop.*"

"Take it easy, Tom," Dylan said, going to him.

Tom shrugged him off. "I'm just saying what we all know deep down. Whoever killed Abbott is desperate. And if they're desperate enough to kill once, they're desperate enough to kill again." Tom looked at Ellery. "I don't know what I'd do in your place, but it seems to me we all know what *that* person will do."

"I didn't ask for any of this," Ellery said. "I just don't want to go to jail for something I didn't do."

Tom nodded curtly. He turned to Dylan. "Night. Thanks for the hospitality."

"I'm not even sure what just happened," Greta said to the room at large.

Dylan said, "You're sure you don't want to finish the game, Tom? Word of honor, we won't discuss crimes past or present."

"No. I really do have an early start tomorrow," Tom said.

"Night, everybody," Libby called, much subdued, as they went out through the front door.

Janet and Sandy left a few minutes later—Ellery promising Sandy he'd be by to pick up Watson within half an hour—and Greta departed on their heels.

"Speaking of Skull House," Mr. Starling said conversationally as Dylan closed the front door behind them, "legend says there are secret passages within the house leading down to the beach. They were used for smuggling brandy and rum back in John Mansfield's day."

"I heard that too," Dylan said, "but as far as I know, no one actually ever found any of these passages. Not even the Tideworths, and they lived there for half a century."

"It would make sense, though," Ellery said. "A lot of these original mansions have secret passages and hidden rooms. Captain's Seat does."

He was thinking that it was more than possible the Tideworths had found the passages but kept the secret...secret.

"Does it?" Dylan asked in surprise.

"Yeah. Well, I don't know about secret passages, but I've found two hidden rooms. They're nothing fancy. More like hidden closets, really."

Mr. Starling said, "As a matter of fact, there's an old network of tunnels beneath the village."

"*What?*" Ellery and Dylan chorused, staring at him.

Mr. Starling seemed equally surprised. "It's a matter of record."

"I never heard that," Dylan said.

"The village was established by pirates *for* pirates. It's not named Farmer's Grove, is it?" Mr. Starling asked tartly.

Dylan said, "I need to hang out at the Historical Society more."

He was joking, but Mr. Starling was not when he said, "If you want to know this village's many secrets, you only have to ask Nora Sweeny. She's a walking, talking Encyclopedia."

"Are the tunnels still used for anything?" Ellery asked.

"No. In the days of the Cold War they were stocked with provisions and blankets. Our mayor back then lived in fear the Russians were coming." Mr. Starling chuckled. "Most of the tunnels are gated now, I believe. Wouldn't want any of these young hooligans getting up to their mischief down there."

"Do the tunnels beneath the village connect to homes outside Pirate's Cove?" Ellery asked.

"No, no. But I think there are homes within the village with cellars opening onto the tunnels."

Dylan muttered, "It's a whole new perspective on the concept of wine cellar. Speaking of which, did either of you want another drink?"

Ellery shook his head. "I should be going. I still have to pick Watson up before I drive home."

"There's a painting of Mansfield's ship the *Golden Fancy* in your bookstore," Mr. Starling informed Ellery.

"You're kidding. I didn't know that."

"It's the big galleon on the wall by the True Crime section."

Ellery and Dylan exchanged looks. Dylan said, "Stanley, you're a treasure trove of information tonight."

"It's those blue cocktails," Mr. Starling confessed. "They pack a wallop."

Dylan chuckled.

Ellery went to get his jacket. When he returned to the dining room, Dylan said to Mr. Starling, "Tell Ellery what you just told me."

Mr. Starling said, "Your aunt Eudora was the one person in Pirate's Cove whose knowledge of this village rivaled Nora's. Have you been through her books and papers yet?"

"No," Ellery admitted. "My focus has been on the bookstore. I've only recently started to work on the house."

"Stanley said some of those books are from the 1700s," Dylan added. "You could have some valuable first editions in that collection."

Ellery hadn't even considered that possibility. The truth was, the sight of that enormous, gloomy room, the musty smell of all those leather-bound volumes crumbling to dust, had been enough to make him close the double doors again and consign Great-great-great-aunt Eudora's personal library to the bottom of his To Do list. If her personal papers were in anything like the shape of her business papers, he had a large and thankless task ahead of him.

Mr. Starling said, "You never know. The answer to some of your questions might lie in one of Eudora's books."

It was hard to imagine what those particular questions might be, but Ellery said thanks and he'd be sure to have a look.

Mr. Starling left not long after, and Ellery and Dylan chatted a little about how the play had gone on Sunday evening. Ellery again declined another drink.

"Tom was in a weird mood tonight," Dylan said, walking Ellery to the front door. "Don't take anything he said too seriously."

"I won't," Ellery promised. But in fact, he thought Tom had largely been correct—and that he'd be a fool *not* to take his warning seriously.

CHAPTER FIFTEEN

Mr. Starling had been right. Those blue cocktails did pack a wallop.

Ellery arrived at work Tuesday morning ever so slightly hungover and wincing each time Watson barked at someone passing the shop's large bay windows—which seemed to be every two and a half minutes.

"You look a mite peaked, dearie," Nora informed Ellery, bringing him two aspirin and a mug of black coffee.

"Thanks, Nora." Ellery managed not to guzzle down the lifesaving fluid, restraining himself to a couple of civilized mouthfuls. He shuddered as the hot liquid hit his empty stomach, but after a second or two he felt marginally better—at least until Watson started barking at the sight of Jack Carson standing out on the pier, talking with someone.

Once upon a time, Jack would have been on his way to see Ellery. They'd spend a pleasant half hour having coffee and chatting. It had been a great way to start the day. Until Jack had stopped coming by, Ellery hadn't realized how much he'd looked forward to those a.m. visits.

If Jack had pulled away after Brandon's murder, Ellery could have understood it. But Jack's withdrawal predated that, and it still hurt. He tried not to dwell on it, but he was also confused because he could have sworn Jack had enjoyed their evening out as much as he had.

Anyway.

Life went on.

Eventually Jack finished doing whatever he was doing, and strode back to where he'd parked, a little way up from the Crow's Nest. As he neared the bookshop, he must have heard Watson's frantic barking because he looked over—and of course caught Ellery staring out the window at him.

Ellery raised a hand in greeting.

Jack raised a hand in greeting.

Jack kept walking.

Watson kept barking.

Ellery went into his office and began figuring out how he was going to pay his bills without any sales.

Shortly after noon, Nora popped her head in and said, "I was just speaking to Nan on the phone. She says she doesn't have any guests booked into the Seacrest Inn until the weekend."

"That's nice," Ellery replied, still thinking about his balance sheets. He realized Nora was giving him a meaningful look. "*Isn't* it nice?"

"It could be useful," Nora said, "if you decided to have a late lunch at the Inn. Nan prepares a delicious crab salad, and she bakes her own biscuits too!"

"Ah." Ellery cocked his head. "Does it bother you at all that you're setting up your own niece?"

Nora sniffed. "You're not exactly the KGB, dearie. Why don't you take a break from the paperwork and have a nice chat with Nan? She'd love to see you, I know."

"Sure, until I start grilling her." But Ellery was more than ready for a break. The numbers in his ledger were not promising, and judging by the morning's business, unlikely to improve anytime soon. Partly that was seasonal, and partly that was Sue Lewis. It was tempting to forgo Nan's crab salad and pay Sue a visit instead, but he didn't want to get thrown in jail for making the threats he was very much afraid would pour out of him the next time he came face-to-face with the owner and editor-in-chief of the *Scuttlebutt Weekly*.

He'd always considered himself a peaceable man, but his feelings toward Sue were increasingly antagonistic. So much so, that if something seriously unfortunate were to befall Ms. Lewis, he wasn't sure he'd be able to summon much sympathy.

He put his paperwork away, grabbed his car keys, and told Nora he'd be driving out to North Point to have lunch at the Seacrest Inn.

"Don't worry about rushing back," Nora instructed him. "Watson and I have everything under control."

Ellery patted Watson goodbye, urged Nora to ring him if anything came up, and went out to his parking space in the alley behind the bookshop. It took a couple of tries to get the VW started. It was a little temperamental, and Jack was always reminding him to take it into Robertson's for a tune-up. Eventually, the navy bug sputtered into life, and Ellery set out for North Point, refusing to fret over the fact that Jack would not be nagging him about car repairs anymore. Surely that was more of a silver lining?

As Nora had predicted, the cute greenhouse-style café attached to the inn was empty, and Nan seemed delighted to see him.

"Ellery! Are you here for lunch? I was going to give up and close for the day. Gosh, we're having some lovely weather, aren't we? Last weekend we had a slew of holidaymakers at the inn. A lovely couple came up from Connecticut and brought both sets of parents and all their kids and their kids spouses and stepkids. We nearly had a full house."

"That's great. Nora was telling me about the crab salad and your homemade biscuits, and I thought maybe I'd treat myself and drive out for lunch."

"You deserve it," Nan said warmly. "I don't know what Sue Lewis's problem is, but no one with half a brain could think you had anything to do with that writer's death."

So much for trying to tell himself a lot of people in the village probably had no idea he was suspected of Brandon's murder.

Nan ushered him into the bright café with its white and black diamond floor and a zillion sparkling windows offering a breathtaking view of the blue sky and bluer harbor.

Ellery sat down in a red leather booth. Nan handed him a menu and said, "It's the first time I've seen you since the play opened. Gosh, it's *so* funny."

"Oh. Er, thank you."

"I haven't laughed that hard in years."

He smiled weakly, handed her back the menu, and said, "I'm already sold on the crab salad."

"Perfect!" I'll put your order in and be right back. Nan vanished into the kitchen but reappeared within seconds with iced water, a small basket of still-warm homemade biscuits, and two small pots of honey and maple syrup.

"This is amazing," Ellery said, slathering butter and honey on one of the fluffy biscuits.

"We get our honey from the Storti apiary on the back of the island."

Ellery, mouth full of flaky biscuit, warm butter, and sweet honey, nodded enthusiastically. He was thinking that it really wasn't any easier to question Nan than it had been to question Mariah. In fact, it was harder because he knew and liked Nan.

But he was in luck, because Nan sat down in the booth across from him, leaned forward across the chrome-plated table, and said, "Is Jack narrowing in on a suspect yet?"

"Jack's not leading the investigation. Detective Lansing is."

"What? Why on earth would Jack hand such an important case to George Lansing?" Nan's expression changed. "*Oh*. Right. Because you guys are..." She crossed her fingers—which frankly, pretty much summed up the extent of Ellery's relationship with Jack. *Good luck with that!*

He said quickly, "Oh, no. No, Jack and I are just friends."

She gave a merry little laugh. "Sure you are!"

"No, really. Just friends."

Nan's face fell. "That's too bad. I thought— I had the impression— *Hm*."

That little reflective *hm* made him uneasy. It was the sound girl sleuths since time began have made when something doesn't quite sit right with them.

More to head her off than anything else, he blurted, "Do you think Brandon's death could have anything to do with what happened at Skull House twenty years ago?"

Nan blinked at him like that did not compute. She said doubtfully, "Brandon?"

"Brandon Abbott. The writer who bought Skull House."

"Oh, him. I forgot his name." Her bright blue eyes met Ellery's uneasily. "Why would you think that?"

In a moment of inspiration, Ellery said, "There's a curse on Skull House, right?"

Nan's lips parted in surprise. "Well, yes, but you surely don't believe *that*?"

Ellery shrugged.

Nan said vaguely, "I don't know. It seems unlikely to me. Let me see how your order's coming along." She jumped up and disappeared into the kitchen once more.

Ellery had another butter-and-honey-soaked biscuit and tried to think of a more subtle approach. Like her aunt Nora, Nan loved to gossip, but as a business owner, she had learned to be a little more cautious, a little more discreet in her confidences.

In a couple of minutes, Nan returned, saying, "I never asked what you wanted to drink. What would you like?"

"Coffee would be great." He had another long evening ahead. The Silver Sleuths Book Club met every Tuesday evening. Usually he left the Silver Sleuths to Nora, but seeing that Nora and Mrs. Nelson planned to drag the club into investigating real-life crimes, he figured he'd better be there.

"Coffee it is!" Nora darted away again, and Ellery sighed.

The next time Nora reemerged, she had his salad. She set the plate in front of Ellery.

"That looks delicious," he said.

She smiled, and he could tell from her body language—something you learned to be very conscious of in acting—that she was divided about whether to stay and talk or retreat yet again.

"The Monday Night Scrabblers got together last night," Ellery said at random. "It was kind of a strange meeting. Or maybe it just seemed like it to me because I'm an outsider."

"You're not an outsider," Nan said. "There have been Pages on Buck Island since the beginning."

"Sure, but I've only been here a few months. I know it's not quite the same thing, and people might not be comfortable talking in front of me. Janet and Tom and Sandy all grew up together on the island. I didn't realize that until Skull House came up and they started discussing whether Brandon's murder could be connected to what happened to Steve Robertson. It was almost like the three of them were speaking in code."

"Are they all part of that club?" Nan asked absently, and moved away again. However, this time she came right back, holding the coffeepot.

As though there had been no interruption, Ellery said, "I guess it's still a sensitive subject. Tom got upset and walked out. I'm not sure why." *Whoo, boy.* And he accused Nora of being a gossip?

Nan said nothing. She poured coffee for Ellery, turned, then abruptly sat down across from him in the booth.

"I was friends with Becky," she said softly, earnestly. "We all were. It was a long time ago, but it still hurts."

"I can imagine," Ellery said. "You were all so young. It would have been shocking at any age, but for a group of college kids—"

"Janet wasn't even in college yet. She wasn't out of high school." Nan bit her lip. "I don't see how there could be any connection between what happened back then and what happened to that writer. I know how hard it must be for you with Sue Lewis pointing the finger at you again, and I don't blame you for looking into it. You solved Trevor's murder. Everyone knows that."

"Actually, I don't think Jack would agree."

Nan smiled faintly, but she wasn't really listening. "It isn't that there's any mystery. It's that we all feel to blame for what happened. We all feel guilty. We know we should have done something, but hindsight is twenty-twenty. At the time, we thought..." Her gaze was troubled. "I'm not even sure. That it wasn't our business? That this was how adults handled things? I don't know. I've spent twenty years wondering what we could have done. In the end, I'm not sure it matters. There isn't any changing it. Two people died that night. One of them was my best friend." Tears shone in her eyes.

"I'm so sorry."

Nan nodded. "I know. You're a nice guy. Aunt Nora says your heart is softer than a coffee cabinet."

"That's... I don't hear that a lot." Ellery was confused until he recalled that a coffee cabinet was a coffee flavored milkshake unique to Rhode Island.

"I knew both Becky and Steve. We grew up together. I would never have thought it would end like that."

"I spoke to Steve's mother," Ellery admitted. "She seems to think it was all Becky's fault."

"Of course she does. Mrs. Robertson knew as much about who Steve really was as I know about quantum physics."

"I see."

"No," Nan said quickly. "I don't mean it like that. Steve wasn't a bad guy. He really wasn't. He was just your typical jock. Arrogant. Full of himself. But that wasn't completely his fault. His parents treated him like a prince. His coaches treated him like God's gift to sports. And girls had been throwing themselves at him since the sixth grade."

"But not Becky."

"No. Not Becky. I think Steve had a crush on her all the way through school, but Becky just wasn't interested. They were friends in junior high, but once they got to high school, they never stopped arguing. Steve just couldn't see that Becky wasn't who he wanted her to be. And she wasn't interested in him. *At all.* In fact, she always liked older guys."

That caught Ellery's interest. Finally. A new piece of information. "Older guys? What older guys? Like here on the island?"

"Nobody serious," Nan said. "Well."

"Well what?"

Nan shook her head. "I shouldn't have. That was all over and done."

"What was?"

Nan was still shaking her head. "I never knew the details. Never knew the guy's name. It was ancient history even back then."

Ellery let it go for the time being. After the previous night, he was trying to polish his interrogation technique. "Were a lot of girls jealous of Becky?"

Nan's forehead wrinkled as she thought it over. "Maybe? Where Steve was concerned. But Becky wasn't... She was really pretty, but it was that quiet kind of prettiness. Not showy. And she was super smart, but again, it wasn't the kind of smart that wins awards or big scholarships. She always knew what she wanted. She always knew who she was. Even when we were really little. Which sounds so silly, but it's true."

"Was she manipulative? Was she—"

"Becky?" Nan laughed. "That's Mrs. Robertson talking. *No.* Becky was the least manipulative girl I've ever met." Nan's eyes started to get a little misty in remembrance. "She was special. She was going to do interesting things, important things. She was going to make a difference in the world. I really believe that."

Through archeology? But okay. People had loved Becky. Nan had loved Becky. Becky had been a girl who knew her own mind, who chose her star and followed it. Sometimes, who knew why, that kind of self-knowledge, independence, call it what you would, bugged other people. Especially people who wanted to control you. People like Steve?

"You said Steve wasn't a bad guy, but isn't it true that most people believe Becky was defending herself that night?"

"Ye-ess." Nan sounded doubtful. "Honestly, it was hard to believe. Steve wasn't mean. He wasn't violent. Well, off the football field. But there really wasn't any other explanation. Becky wouldn't have just attacked him for no good reason."

"Did anyone actually see what happened?"

"No one saw anything, but it wasn't hard to put two and two together. Steve was drinking—he always drank more when Becky was around—and he was more jealous and more insecure after she went away to college. That night he was being a total jerk. T-someone told him to take a walk and cool down, and he did. That was the last time any of us saw him alive. He was walking away from the house, walking along the cliff."

"But he didn't fall off the cliff."

"No. About an hour later we found him dead in the master bedchamber." She shuddered. "His head was bashed in. It was…horrible."

"I'm sure it was. What about Becky? Where was she?"

"When Steve walked off, Becky went to get another drink. That was it. No one ever saw her again."

"Wait. At *all*?"

"I never saw her again."

"But someone must have seen her at some point."

"No. We've compared notes over the years. We're all agreed. No one saw her after that."

"When did Steve return to the house?"

"No one really remembers."

"So no one saw Becky after she went to get a drink, and no one remembers Steve coming back to the house, and no one actually saw any part of the final confrontation between Becky and Steve?"

"Right."

"Doesn't that strike you as strange?"

Nan looked uncomfortable. "We were all drinking and, um, some of us were all fooling around. It's a huge house. There were a lot of places to go if you wanted to be private."

"How many kids were at the party?"

"Thirty or so."

"*Thirty?*"

"Yes. It was spring break, so there were kids on the island who didn't live here, who were just visiting or had come for the weekend. Flyers were passed around all over town. Every college-age kid who walked off the ferry that Friday got one." Nan looked apologetic, as though somehow it was her fault. "It was a big party."

Thirty kids. Yikes. No wonder the thing was still a mystery. Those Pirate's Cove teens could have accidentally invited a serial-killer-in-training to their party. Half the suspects had probably left the island within a day or so. This would be impossible to solve.

And yet, the crime…the victim, the perpetrator, the motive, the modus operandi…none of that was random. None of that seemed like it could be accidental or happenstance.

"Even so," Ellery said. "It just seems odd. There had been some run-in with Steve, obviously, since he was told to take a hike. Then Becky goes to get another drink and vanishes. Didn't anyone wonder when she didn't come back with her drink?"

Nan's eyes filled with tears again. "I've asked myself a million times why I didn't check on her. But I was—there was a boy I liked—and I figured Becky was taking a little time-out. She loved the house. She loved exploring it. She knew the house better than any of us. She'd been there a few times. She was always looking for the supposed secret passages. So I just figured she was off exploring. That would have been like her."

"Did anyone ever look for her afterward?"

"Of course. Four of us sneaked back every night for a week and tried to find where she was hiding. But by then she must have…left the island."

"So you do think she left the island."

Nan hesitated. "I did at the time. I don't anymore. I think she would have contacted me."

"Then you think—" Ellery began tentatively.

Nan finished his thought. She said steadily, "I think she's dead."

CHAPTER SIXTEEN

"*I* don't think she's dead," Mrs. Nelson said.

It was Tuesday night, and the Silver Sleuths Book Club was in progress. However, that week's reading selection—Diana Killian's *Corpse Pose*—had been discarded in order to discuss what Nora persisted in calling "their case."

"Then where is she?" Mr. Starling demanded, as though expecting Mrs. Nelson to produce the culprit from her voluminous handbag.

Mrs. Nelson pointed meaningfully to the empty chair within their circle.

The remaining three members, and Ellery, stared at the chair where Mrs. Smith usually sat.

"What are we looking at? I don't see anyone," Mr. Starling objected.

"She means Jane Smith," Mrs. Ferris explained.

"Hmmm..." Nora frowned, considering this.

"Okay, stop." Ellery rose. "You guys, this is

slander. You can't start accusing people of murder just because—"

"I'm not accusing her of *murder*," Mrs. Nelson protested. "It would surely have been justifiable homicide."

Mr. Starling and Mrs. Ferris nodded eagerly in agreement.

Ellery gaped at them, turned to Nora, who still had that thoughtful expression on her face. "This is not okay. You can't—"

"We can hardly discuss the case and not mention any names," Nora pointed out.

"Which is why you need to stop discussing the case. For one thing, I don't need a lawsuit for defamation, or whatever it would be, filed against the Crow's Nest. For another, you have no idea how horrible it is to have people suspecting you of murder and not be able to defend yourself."

"You're taking this too personally, dearie," Nora said kindly. She even patted his arm.

"That's the very reason we're tackling this case. We're trying to help you, Ellery," Mrs. Nelson said. "We're trying to clear your name."

"Which is…kind, I guess. Which I appreciate. But this isn't the way."

"What way do you suggest?" Mr. Starling asked. "*You're* poking around, asking questions. Everyone in the village knows you're trying to solve this crime. How fair is it to cut us out of the investigation when it was our idea to begin with?"

"I'm not— This isn't— I don't think you realize the potential dan—"

Nora cut in, "Hermione, I admit my thoughts have been running in the same direction. Why do *you* suspect Jane Smith—aside, of course, from the fact that *Jane Smith* is obviously an alias."

"First of all, her obvious efforts to cast suspicion from herself and onto Ellery."

"She's a gossip," Ellery protested. "You're *all* gossips. How is her gossiping any different?"

"She went to the police about your argument with Abbott," Nora answered. "That's the first difference."

Okay, that was news. Ellery hadn't realized that Mrs. Smith had gone out of her way to report his disagreement with Brandon. And, now that he thought about it, there was something a little…off about Mrs. Smith. Something sneaky. Something furtive. Or was he letting the suspicions of the others influence him? Because until this moment, such an idea had never occurred to him.

"She's too old," he objected, sitting down again.

"No," Mrs. Ferris said eagerly. "She's not. She's much younger than she looks. I once managed to catch a glimpse of her driver's license in the grocery store, and she's only thirty-eight!"

"*Exactly* the age Rebecca would be now," Mrs. Nelson said with satisfaction.

"She's only lived on the island ten years," Nora said. "She has no family here. No friends. No one knew her at all before she arrived. Why *would* she choose to live here? Out of all the places in the world where one could live?"

"Because you're all so warm and welcoming to a stranger?" muttered Ellery.

"And she's very secretive," Mrs. Nelson said.

"I've noticed that too," Mrs. Ferris said. "She never speaks of her past or her family or—"

Ellery groaned and put his face in his hands.

"Ellery, dearie," Nora said with some exasperation, "why don't you take little Watson for a walk? That *Treasury of Sherlock Holmes* is going to be completely unsalable if he continues chewing on it."

Ellery jumped up and went to rescue the 1955 blue and gold collector's edition. Watson wagged his tail and smiled up at him, delighted to show off his workmanship.

"Want to go for a walk?" Ellery asked, and Watson abandoned the book and began to run in circles around him.

The Silver Sleuths were discussing whether Mrs. Smith could have had plastic surgery when Ellery and Watson, now on his leash, stepped out into the damp night and closed the door to the Crow's Nest behind them.

It would be hypocritical to criticize the Silver Sleuths for doing the very thing he was: trying to figure out if Brandon's murder could possibly be tied to the earlier tragedy at Skull House.

And he could understand why they—Nora, in particular—might want to believe Rebecca Witherspoon had survived that terrible night.

He knew they were trying to help. And he could use all the help he could get.

They knew a lot more about the island and each and every citizen of Pirate's Cove than he probably ever would.

Even so. *Yeesh.*

It was a relief to get out of there, to look at the faintly twinkling stars and feel the cool salty air against his face. He walked briskly down the narrow streets, Watson pulling at his leash, the puppy not walking so much as making rabbit-like leaps through triangles of lamplight.

Ellery didn't think Mrs. Smith was a very likely candidate for murderer, even if she was maybe a little odd. Heck, everyone in Pirate's Cove was a little odd.

No, he kept coming back to Nan's comment earlier that day about an older man, an earlier relationship in Rebecca's life. He had tried to press Nan on it, but she hadn't been willing to say anything more. And when he'd tried to bring up the possibility with the Silver Sleuths… Well, that had gone completely off the rails.

They'd dismissed the idea and instead turned their spotlight on Jane Smith.

It was interesting the way people either demonized or idealized Rebecca. Surely, the truth had to fall somewhere in the middle? An eighteen-year-old kid was bound to make some mistakes, however smart and mature for her age she was. And the same could be said for Steve Robertson.

By then, Ellery and Watson had turned onto Wallace Street. He spotted the old Marchmont theater and was surprised to see a light on in the basement office. Dylan must have been working late.

On impulse, Ellery crossed the street to the theater. He was in the mood for some company, and despite Dylan's flair for the dramatic, he was extremely practical and a pretty good judge of character. Ellery wanted to run one or two theories by him.

Seeing that Jack was no longer available for brainstorming, let alone idle chitchat.

He went to the side entrance and used the key Dylan had given him for those evening rehearsals when Dylan had been running late.

The door swung silently open on well-oiled hinges (the better not to disturb the players), and Ellery stepped inside. The usual theater scents tickled his nostrils: one-million-year-BC popcorn, old upholstery and older draperies, sawdust... The stair and aisle lights glowed greenish in the dark, and he didn't bother to turn on the switch, instead tugging Watson from his cautious investigations, and trotting down the steps to the below-stage floor of the theater.

He wasn't at all nervous to be there when the building was empty. He grew up in theaters like the Marchmont. His mother taught drama to high schoolers. His father was an acting coach. He felt perfectly at home heading downstairs.

The overhead lights were on. He paused at the foot of the stairs, scanning the familiar walkway. The corridor of dressing rooms was T-shaped, with the women's dressing room on the right and the men's on the left. His gaze fell on the long gallery of dusty framed photos, and he smiled faintly. The Scallywags had been treading the boards since the theater had first opened in 1898.

For a moment he studied these glimpses of stage performances through the decades, grinning when he recognized a familiar face beneath the wigs and grease paint. Nora in a flaming red wig and witch costume...Dylan, light years younger, with dark-brown hair and a devilish smile. Sue Lewis was there too, holding up what appeared to be a bloody dagger—no doubt about to plunge it into someone's unsuspecting back. Was that Janet in Elizabethan costume? Yep, there she was again with Tom Tulley. He made a very convincing Viking. Neither was still active in the Scallywags, but Cyrus Jones was. That picture of him, looking fit and surprisingly handsome, had to have been taken long before he had been elected mayor. Oh, and there was Libby, adorable in pigtails, Mary Janes, and a Shirley Temple wig.

Next to the photo of Libby was a blank square on the wall where a framed picture had been removed— and next to it, another white square. The next photos were several years earlier and featured people Ellery didn't recognize at all.

That was weird. He had never noticed any gaps in the gallery before.

He studied the ghostly square outlines and suddenly remembered Nora mentioning that Rebecca had been active in a drama club. Ellery had been assuming high-school theater, but maybe, even likely, Rebecca had been a member of the Scallywags.

Did one of these young, unfamiliar smiles belong to Rebecca?

His gaze was drawn irresistibly back to the two white squares in the long line of framed memories.

Or had Rebecca been in one of the now-missing photographs?

But why remove her photos? It wasn't like—

Right. Of course. It wouldn't be about Rebecca's captured image. It would be about whoever had shared those frames with her. But what a foolish move. The decision to remove the photos revealed far more than the photos themselves could ever have.

Ellery's heart began to thump with excitement. Would Dylan remember who had been in those missing photos?

He turned to continue toward the office where Dylan was working. He had a glimpse of the fire exit, a pair of plywood painted trees leaning against the wall, and a figure in a dark hoodie coming around the corner just as the hallway went black.

Watson began to bark.

For a frozen second Ellery wasn't sure what had happened, wasn't sure what had happened to the lights, wasn't sure if he had really seen what he thought he had, and then the significance of that approaching figure—and the deep, unfamiliar growl in Watson's voice—registered.

He bent, scooped up Watson, who began to wriggle furiously, and ran for the stairs.

He overshot them, had to turn around, and to his horror, collided with a solid, definitely male, body. Something slammed across his shoulder so hard, he let go of Watson. The pain was dizzying. He thought his arm must be broken, but had the presence of mind to drop into a crouch, groping with his good arm for the puppy, who was barking furiously, just out of reach.

Head swimming, Ellery crawled forward, frantically feeling for the leash, finding it at last, hauling Watson, head over paws, to him—and at that moment, his attacker fell over him.

Fell. Over him.

Was this for real?

The other man hit the ground with an *ooof* that Ellery thought was vaguely familiar, even as he clutched Watson to him, staggering to his feet once more and sprinting blindly up the stairs.

His lungs were burning, his heart hammering, his muscles shaking as he reached the house floor. That was more adrenaline overload—fear—than exertion; he was in very good shape—and desperately hoping to stay that way.

He burst out through the curtained entrance and saw the dim outline of row upon row of empty seats, the empty orchestra pit, the empty stage. Watson was still wiggling, still whining, but Ellery clung to him as he charged for the side door and banged out into the cold night.

The door seemed to hang motionless for a nerve-racking eternity, as though waiting for Ellery's assailant to catch up with him. Ellery stared wildly up and down the block.

The street was completely empty. The shops all closed and shuttered. There were no cars. There were no pedestrians. There was no help to be had, and he dropped Watson to the ground, hanging onto his leash and jogging away from the brick building.

"Come on, Watson. Come on, puppy," he panted. His shoulder was throbbing in time to the pound of his feet on the pavement. Watson, deciding this was a fantastic new game, soon outdistanced him, dragging Ellery along behind him.

CHAPTER SEVENTEEN

"I'm not saying I don't believe you. Here." Jack handed Ellery a plastic bag of ice wrapped in a faded-blue dish towel. Jack knelt, placing an ice cube on the floor for Watson, who promptly pawed it, sending it shooting across the floor of Jack's office.

Ellery pressed the ice pack against bare shoulder. He had a long dark bruise across his shoulder, but his arm was not broken after all. Thank God for that. He muttered, "You just think I'm letting my imagination run away with me."

Jack half sat on his desktop, facing Ellery. "No. You didn't imagine being attacked. But I think you're jumping to conclusions." Despite his words, Jack's tone was more gentle than usual.

The police station was closed at nine o'clock at night, but Ellery knew Jack often worked late, and he'd taken a chance after escaping from the theater on Wallace Street. Sure enough, Jack had been inside, coming to answer his frantic buzzing.

Ellery had poured out the whole story of going to the theater, seeing the downstairs light and thinking Dylan must be working late, and then noticing the missing photographs at about the same time the intruder had noticed him.

Jack had heard him out, and then they'd driven over to the theater together, only to find it locked and dark and empty. Which really wasn't surprising. As Ellery had pointed out, the intruder would hardly hang around after Ellery escaped.

And he did believe he'd had a narrow escape.

Jack… Not so much. Jack had been troublingly noncommittal throughout. He had insisted on Ellery returning to the station and filing a report—although, in fairness, when he'd seen the bruise on Ellery's shoulder, his eyes had turned flinty and his mouth had thinned to a hard line.

He said now, "It looks like he hit you with a crowbar, which may be how he got into the building."

"Then you agree it wasn't Dylan who came after me. Dylan would have used his own key."

"Would he?" Jack's tone was grim. "Not if he has any brains. He'd want it to look like a break-in."

"It wasn't Dylan," Ellery said stubbornly.

Jack sighed. He'd had a long day too, no question, and Ellery was probably jumping up and down on his last nerve, but he said patiently, "You didn't see his face. He didn't speak, so you can't identify his voice."

"I think I'd—"

"Dylan's the right age to fit the older-man profile. He's got a reputation with the ladies. He was active with the Scallywags at the time Rebecca would have been a member. He knows the theater inside and out. But because you think he's your friend, you're convinced it couldn't have been Dylan."

"Dylan wouldn't try to kill me."

"Well, seeing that he didn't kill you, maybe he wasn't trying that hard."

"Dylan's not a murderer."

"Ellery." Jack sounded pained.

"I know, I know how you think. But he's not the type."

Jack gave a little shake of his head and stared ceilingward in a *God give me strength* gesture.

"Okay, you believe everyone is the type, given the right set of circumstances. Well, these wouldn't have been the right set of circumstances."

"How could you possibly know?" Jack was getting exasperated. "You weren't there that night at Skull House. Apparently, even the people who were there, weren't there. So—"

"Dylan would have had a million opportunities to remove those photos. Why would he wait till—"

"Late at night when no one was around? Seems like a good idea to me." Jack met Ellery's gaze and grimaced. "But nope. You're convinced the man we're looking for is—"

"Cyrus."

Jack winced, though it wasn't the first time in the last half hour Ellery had offered this theory. "The mayor."

"Yes."

"Doting dad, doting grandfather, pillar of the community, regular churchgoer. That Cyrus?"

"You're the one who thinks everyone is capable of murder."

Jack gave him a long look.

Ellery said, "Jack, Dylan's in great shape. I'm not sure I could have gotten away so easily from him. But whoever tackled me in the theater wasn't as physically fit. He sounded winded on the steps when he was coming after me. He was shorter than me but a lot wider. Solid. Dylan's shorter than me, but he's trim and muscular. And I know Dylan's aftershave. This guy smelled like cigarettes."

Jack's gaze sharpened. "Cyrus doesn't smoke."

"No, but *Felix* does. He used to sneak out to smoke during rehearsals. And Felix wears oversize dark hoodies."

Jack grunted noncommittally, but he leaned back to jot a couple of notes down on the pad sitting on his desk blotter. "This is really thin," he commented.

"I know. And the thing is, I like Cyrus. He's been kind to me and supportive of the bookshop. I don't want to think he's capable of any of this stuff. But you did say when that true-crime series tried to film a segment on Skull House, the town fathers nixed it. And we all know Cyrus is the real force behind the town council. And when Mariah Robertson complained to the town council about my visiting her, Cyrus came to see me and dropped a few subtle reminders about my business license. Doesn't that seem a little extreme?"

"Maybe."

"When I saw that photo of him... Twenty years ago he wasn't grandfatherly Cyrus. He was a reasonably attractive thirty-year-old guy who got married right out of high school and liked theater and—by the way, he's not a bad actor either. He's not as good as Felix, but he's decent. He could tell a convincing lie if he had to."

Jack stopped making notes and sighed. "I know you're trying to be helpful."

"But those are all things that could factor in."

Jack gave a half-laugh. "Are they? Well, at least this isn't coming via tiles on a Scrabble board."

Ouch. Ellery scowled. "For your information, it's the same mental process. I just use Scrabble as a mechanism for my subconscious to sift through a bunch of cues and clues and sort out the possibilities."

"Don't ruin it," Jack said. He tossed his pencil down and straightened. "Okay, listen up."

Ellery waited, trying not to feel defensive.

"I'm not going to deny that you've come up with useful information, especially everything you learned during your conversation with Nan today. I've known Nan for years, and I had no idea she was at Skull House that night. I'd have bet money she wasn't." Jack's expression was wry. "I'm not even going to deny that some of your insights are potentially...interesting."

"Potentially interesting?" Ellery questioned. "So...not interesting yet but maybe one day?"

"Don't be a smartass," Jack said. He glanced down, noticed Watson chewing the feet of his coatrack and growled, "Watson!"

Watson sat up, cocking his head. One of his ears tipped forward and one tipped back.

Jack rubbed his face. "I will relay all this information to Detective Lansing tomorrow, and I'll strongly encourage him to follow up with you on this angle."

"Which angle?" Ellery was not being sarcastic. He was afraid he was hoping for too much, afraid Jack was not actually saying what he thought he was saying.

Jack said very patiently, "The angle of Brandon Abbott's murder being connected to that of Steve Robertson." He added bleakly, "And, very likely, the murder of Rebecca Witherspoon."

Right. Because if Ellery's speculations were correct, there could be little doubt that poor Rebecca too was dead.

Ellery nodded.

"But the sleuthing stops here." Jack's eyes were somber. "You were lucky tonight, Ellery. Things could easily have gone another way."

"Yeah, but I wasn't sleuthing when I went into the theater," Ellery protested. "I was just hoping to talk to Dylan."

"Among other things, about everything you'd learned from Nan."

"Er…"

"*Exactly.*"

Ellery met Jack's steady gaze and grimaced. "Okay, yes. I promise." After all, his intention had only ever been to dig up enough information to supply an alternative solution to his own suspected guilt. He'd done that. "I'm more than happy to leave this to the police now."

Jack snorted. "That's generous. We'll do our best to live up to your expectations."

Ellery laughed, rose, and handed Jack his ice-pack. "I have every faith in you."

Jack laughed too, and for a few moments it was like it had been before everything got weird between them.

Jack seemed to recall himself. He turned and shuffled a couple of papers on his perfectly tidy desk, and Ellery shrugged back into his shirt, and then more gingerly his jacket.

"Are you okay to drive?" Jack asked.

"Yep."

Jack seemed to hesitate. He said brusquely, "Give me a ring when you get home, so I know you made it safely."

"Uh-oh," Ellery said. "Careful. I'm liable to start thinking you care."

Jack held his gaze. He said, "I do care. So be careful."

"Since you insist." Ellery knelt, snapped Watson's leash back on, and rose.

Neither he nor Jack spoke as they walked through the silent building to the front door. Jack unlocked the glass door, holding it open.

"I can give you a lift if you're nervous about walking back to your car."

"No, it's fine," Ellery said. "What would be the point of coming after me now?"

"Just...stay alert."

"Night." Ellery slipped past him, letting Watson hurry him along. He gave a backward wave over his shoulder without looking around.

* * * * *

The drive from Pirate's Cove felt especially long and especially dark that night.

Ellery had just passed the spot where he had first found Watson—now sleeping peacefully, harnessed in the seat beside him—when all the lights on the VW's dashboard began to flash.

"*Now?*" Ellery protested. "You're choosing now to conk out?"

He still had about ten minutes to Captain's Seat, and he was weighing whether trying to coax the VW a few more miles might wreck the engine once and for all, when the dashboard flickered and went out, along with the engine.

He took his foot off the brake and let the car's momentum roll them to the side of the road, whereupon he quietly, bitterly vented his feelings for a few seconds, ending with a punch on the steering wheel that hurt his hand and did nothing to wake up the VW.

It was not too far to walk—about seven miles—but he wasn't thrilled about making the trek at this time of night and in near total darkness.

Sometimes the bug just needed a few minutes to regain its composure before it started up again.

He sat there for a minute or two, listening to Watson muttering in his sleep—he made the most disconcertingly human noises sometimes—and then Ellery lost patience, opened the car door, and went to check under the hood at the back of the car.

He turned his cell flashlight on, studied the wires, hoses, tanks, rods, and pistons, hoping that something would jump out at him—though not literally—and finally had to concede defeat. Changing tires and oil was about the extent of his mechanic skill set.

Hopefully it was just a short, and when he tried the ignition in a couple of minutes, everything would start again, although he had to admit there had been something very final in those last flashes of dashboard light.

Ellery slammed the hood shut, checked his phone, but he already knew from experience there was no signal along this stretch of road. There was one bright spot. He'd promised to phone Jack when he got home, and Jack, being Jack, would surely come looking for him if he didn't get that call.

He dropped the phone in his pocket, turning at the distant growl of an approaching engine.

Sound carried out here in the middle of nowhere. Was that really headed his way?

Yes. Hallelujah. He could see the twin dots of headlights approaching, high beams slicing across the black ribbon of road, the high hedges and low stone walls.

His heart rose.

One nice thing about the island was no one would ever pass by a stranded motorist without stopping to lend a hand or offer a ride.

He waited by the side of the VW, waving as the headlights of the approaching vehicle drew near. The shining beams partially blinded him, but he could see that it was a car—a black Mercedes—drawing even with his own.

He didn't recognize the car. He wouldn't have recognized almost anyone's car on the island. The passenger side automatic window rolled down, and Ellery bent to look in.

"Thanks for stopping," he began, and then stopped.

Mayor Cyrus Jones sat behind the wheel of the Mercedes. "No trouble, my boy. Is it the engine or a flat tire?" Cyrus's face looked an unearthly green in the glow of the dashboard.

Ellery said, and he was surprised at how normal he sounded, "The engine, I think." He was frantically running through his options and drawing a blank. This could not be a coincidence. Cyrus lived in Pirate's Cove. He did not just happen to be tooling around the countryside at midnight. He had to have been following Ellery, and if he was following Ellery, was it because he knew Ellery was going to have car trouble? Had Cyrus tampered with the VW's engine?

"You'd better hop in. I'll give you a lift home," Cyrus said. There was something terrifying about his normally cheery smile. His lips were pulled back from his teeth, so he looked like he was snarling.

Ellery stepped back from the Mercedes, saying, "Thanks, but no need. I've already phoned Robertson's Garage. A tow truck is on the way." He threw a hopeful look down the road, but there was no miracle speeding his way.

Cyrus made a sound that was part amusement and part impatience. "No, you didn't. You just thanked me for stopping. Get in the car, my boy. Don't be foolish."

"I think getting in the car would be more foolish," Ellery said.

Cyrus shook his head, raised his right hand from the shadows of the passenger seat. The dashboard lights winked off the metal of a short-barreled shot-gun. "Wanna bet?" he said.

There's something paralyzing about having a gun pointed at you.

Ellery pictured turning to run, and instantly imagined seeing the muzzle flash, hearing that terrible *bang*, feeling the bullet tear into him. He couldn't think of any way to get out of range in time. And though he knew it was a fatal mistake climbing into the car with Cyrus, that Cyrus could be planning only one outcome, it felt equally fatal to not get into the car.

In those echoing, endlessly long seconds, he learned that it is human instinct to prolong your life as long as you can, even if it is in minute by minute increments.

Accordingly, he reached for the door handle, opened it, and slid into the passenger seat.

"That's it, there you go," Cyrus said encouragingly.

Ellery pulled shut the door, with a final silent farewell to Watson, whose little nose was sticking up over the side-window ledge of the VW, furiously sniffing the night air.

"Is that a blunderbuss?" he asked Cyrus, at random.

"Yes, but don't worry. It's in perfect working order," Cyrus said. His tongue stuck out a little from between his teeth as he released the brake and concentrated on driving with one hand and pointing the shotgun at Ellery with the other.

The barrel of the blunderbuss wavered in front of Ellery's face. If he tried to grab it, would Cyrus shoot him? Could he push the barrel away from himself, so that the blast could go through the roof of the car? Would that result in a ricochet?

His desperate thoughts were interrupted by Cyrus swearing in frustration. "This isn't going to work!"

"I know," Ellery said. "I've already told Chief Carson everything."

"I don't mean that!" Cyrus jammed on the brakes, and they both lurched forward. Cyrus opened his door, and still pointing the blunderbuss at Ellery, slid out. "Don't try anything funny."

"Not moving a muscle," Ellery said quickly. "See?" He was praying Cyrus didn't force him out of the car and shoot him then and there.

"You get behind the wheel."

Ellery climbed awkwardly behind the wheel, watching through the windshield as Cyrus—aiming the shotgun at him all the while—crossed in front of the car, squinting in the headlights, making his way to the passenger side.

Hit the gas. Run him over. Now. Do it now.

But Ellery couldn't do it. Imagination can be a curse.

Cyrus clambered back into the Mercedes, panting a little. "All right. Drive."

Ellery asked blankly, "Where?"

"Where else?" Cyrus said rather bitterly, "Skull House."

CHAPTER EIGHTEEN

"**Y**ou know, you don't have to do this," Ellery said, just as Noah Street had said in every single one of the six *Happy Halloween* films. At least he knew his lines!

"I wish that was true," Cyrus said. "You have no idea."

"I wasn't lying. I went straight to Chief Carson when I left the theater. I told him everything I know."

Ellery kept his eyes on the dark, empty road, but he was painfully conscious of the gun barrel bobbing a few inches from his head. Sweat prickled along his hairline and beneath his armpits.

Cyrus said indifferently, "Maybe you did, but how much do you really know?"

"Enough, if you think it's worth killing me over."

"You have a point there," Cyrus admitted, sounding so much like his regular self, it was almost eerie.

"So why do this? It's just going to make it worse for you." *Not to mention me.*

Cyrus said wearily, "It's very hard to convict someone of murder without a body. Did you know that? Almost no prosecutor ever wants to go to trial without a body."

Ellery took a wild guess. "You're going to try to hide my body in Skull House like you hid Rebecca's."

"Mm-hm." Cyrus didn't sound even a little surprised that Ellery had put those pieces of the puzzle together.

"So there really are secret passages?"

"Yes. They're practically standard features in these old houses. The Pirate Eight for certain."

The Pirate Eight were the first houses built on Buck Island. All eight homes had started out as pirate fortresses.

Ellery said, "But these are totally different circumstances. By framing Rebecca for murder, you were able to give her a motive for disappearing. No one is going to believe I willingly disappeared. PICO PD is going to come after you."

"Good luck proving anything. It's your word against mine, and you won't be around to talk." Cyrus gave a heavy sigh as though the weight of the world was on his shoulders.

Ellery realized he was wasting his breath. Cyrus was blind to the obvious holes in his plan. He had convinced himself he was going to get away with yet another murder, and with his track record so far, it was easy to see why he thought so, why homicide was getting to be a habit.

They covered another mile of moonlit road, while Ellery racked his brains for some solution, some way out.

"Why did you kill Brandon?" he asked, partly to keep Cyrus talking—he had read somewhere that creating a rapport with your abductor was your best shot of staying alive—but partly because the question haunted him.

Cyrus groaned. "I don't want to talk about it. I am a *good* person, whether you believe that or not. I didn't want *any* of this."

Ellery didn't know what to say to that, but after a minute or two, Cyrus started talking again. Maybe he couldn't help himself.

"He *had* to go. I didn't have any choice there."

"Why?" Ellery thought about it. "Because of the house renovations? Because Rebecca's body was bound to be discovered?"

"That sure didn't help," Cyrus agreed glumly. "I should have blocked that sale, but Nora was never going to let it go. And his books were so stupid; I couldn't see how he'd be a threat. I didn't think he'd really try to do any *real* investigating. It's always some kind of supernatural entity causing trouble in his stories. But I'll be damned if right out of the gate he didn't hit on the fact that Rebecca was having an affair with someone in the bank."

"The bank?"

"I used to be the manager of Pirate's Cove Bank and Trust. Rebecca worked there the summer before she started college." Cyrus muttered something Ellery didn't catch. "He actually sat right here where I'm sitting in this car, joking about whether *I* might have been the guy."

God, Brandon. But that had been Brandon. He had been incapable of keeping his thoughts—or even his imaginings—to himself.

"Was this when Brandon dropped his rental car off?" Ellery said slowly. "You gave him a ride back to Skull House?"

"Yes. I was trying to be nice! I didn't have anything against him."

"But then how did he make that phone call to me that night?"

Cyrus snorted. "He didn't. I did. I made it right before rehearsal, but somehow you didn't get the call until later."

Ellery threw the mayor a quick, disbelieving look. "You were trying to frame me for his murder."

"No, no. Of course not. Well, sort of." Cyrus sounded uncomfortable. "It wasn't personal. I like you, my boy. I always have. But you were the only person who Abbott knew here on the island. How was I to know there would be so much evidence against you? That was just...serendipity."

"Oh, is that the word?" Ellery said bleakly.

"I *am* sorry," Cyrus said. "I didn't plan any of this. I'm a good person. I've done many good things for this community. Should a man's life be judged by one bad mistake?"

Which bad mistake was Cyrus referring to? The affair with a teenaged girl? The murder of that girl and another boy? Brandon's murder? The next murder he was planning to commit?

Ellery said none of that. It would not have been conducive to building rapport. He made himself ask neutrally, "How did you kill him?"

"I hit him over the head. What an idiot he was. He thought I was a possible suspect, yet he let me drive him home, walked into the house with me, even turned his back on me..." The blunderbuss knocked against Ellery's shoulder as Cyrus shrugged.

Ellery flinched. Cyrus said automatically, "Sorry." They were both silent.

Only a few more miles before they reached Skull House... Ellery could think of nothing but crashing the car, and that was liable to kill them both. Maybe once they reached the house, he'd have an opportunity to disarm Cyrus or, failing that, run and hide.

One thing for sure, Cyrus was not comfortable holding a gun. His weapon of choice seemed to be knocking people over the head with whatever was handy. Nor was he much of a planner. All his murders seemed to be crimes of impulse.

Or were they?

"What about the warning notes you sent him?"

Cyrus laughed. "I wrote that note right after I killed him. I crumpled it up, threw it in the corner, and sure enough, you found it."

Sure enough.

When Ellery said nothing, Cyrus spoke, his tone defensive, "I have a family to think of. I have a son. He's not even out of school yet. I have a *granddaughter*. I have to think of them."

"I have family too," Ellery said. "I have a mom and a dad. They're—"

"I can't help that! You should have stayed out of it. I don't know why you didn't. Abbott was horrible to you. Everyone saw it. If you had just left it alone…"

"But I didn't, and now Jack knows everything, so what's the point of killing me? He knows you killed Rebecca, he knows you killed Steve and Brandon, and he'll know you killed me."

"What does it matter if he can't prove it?"

Ellery threw Cyrus a look of disbelief. "You can't really believe that."

"I have to believe it." Cyrus's eyes gleamed in the darkness of the car interior.

They rounded the last hairpin curve in the road, and Pequot Bluffs and the house came into view.

Moonlight gilded its towers, turned the windows silver as the coins on dead men's eyes.

"Come on, come on," Cyrus said. "Don't slow down."

Ellery pressed the accelerator, and they started up the hill toward the mansion.

His heart was pounding so hard he felt sick, and his palms were slick with sweat.

It's now or never, he thought.

Cyrus leaned forward, peering out the windshield. "Is that a car?"

Ellery unobtrusively slid his left hand down the steering wheel and then felt quietly, carefully for the door handle.

Cyrus swore softly. "Is that Jack Carson's—"

At the same moment, Ellery's cell phone rang.

A blast shattered the windshield as Cyrus's finger tightened instinctively on the trigger of his blunderbuss. Ellery didn't waste a second, clutching for the door handle, opening the door, and spilling out onto the dirt road. He rolled away from the tires, scrambling into the brush and wild grass, heart racing a million miles a minute.

Ellery's phone stopped ringing.

Insanely, the song "It's now or never" was running through the back of his mind, over and over.

It's now or never...

It's now or never...

Those were the only lyrics he knew. He didn't even *like* that song.

Somewhere in the distance, an engine roared into life.

The Mercedes veered wildly, went off the road, and started down the shrub-studded embankment. Ellery got on his knees, trying to see what was happening, and to his amazement, he watched the car tip onto its side and slide a few feet.

He didn't wait. He sprang up and ran for the top of the hill, zigzagging as he went.

It's now or never, Elvis caroled.

Ellery was about halfway up when he heard a shot behind him. The sound seemed to blow apart the night. He threw himself into the nearby brush, gulping for breath.

"Stop!" Cyrus shouted breathlessly from a yard or so down the road. "Stop or I'll…shoot."

"You're already shooting," Ellery muttered, wiping his face on his sleeve.

Headlights swept through the dusty, pungent bushes tickling his face, pinpointing Cyrus trudging up the road, blunderbuss raised. Ellery lifted his head and saw blue and red halogen lights cutting a swath through the misty night air. The police SUV gave a couple of loud *WHOOP, WHOOP, WHOOPs!* as it sped down the rough road.

The SUV slid to a tire-crunching halt, positioned between Ellery and Cyrus. The door flew open and Jack stepped out, bracing his arm on the top of the door, aiming his weapon straight at Cyrus.

"Drop it or I'll drop you, Cyrus." Jack's voice was cold and even.

Cyrus wavered for a moment, then dropped his blunderbuss and put his arms up.

"Th-this is all a misunderstanding, Jack," he stammered.

"You okay, Ellery?" Jack called, without turning his head.

Ellery got to his feet. "I'm okay." His voice was almost steady. His heart, not so much.

It's now or never, crooned Elvis.

* * * * *

"If Cyrus said he's a good person one more time, I was going to punch him," Jack said.

"Hey, good people do bad things," Ellery replied lightly.

Not that he didn't still have nightmares about that seemingly endless drive Tuesday night with Cyrus to Skull House.

It was late Sunday afternoon, and Jack had driven out to Captain's Seat to "bring Ellery up to speed" on recent developments in the case against Mayor Cyrus Jones.

He didn't really have to bother. Ellery had heard pretty much every twist and turn of the ongoing tale from the never-ending stream of customers who had dropped by the Crow's Nest that week.

And, of course, there was always Sue Lewis's account in the *Scuttlebutt Weekly* of how Police Chief Carson had single-handedly solved the tragic mystery that had haunted Pirate's Cove for so long.

Ellery knew that once Cyrus had been hauled into the police station, he had started talking, and by all accounts, was *still* talking. Cyrus had admitted to abducting Ellery, murdering Brandon, and killing Steve in a fit of rage when Steve had stumbled upon Cyrus and Rebecca. The only thing Cyrus didn't admit to was murdering Rebecca. He kept insisting that had been an accident, that he had really, truly loved Rebecca and had never meant to harm her.

"Do you believe him?" Ellery asked as he and Jack had coffee in the kitchen Jack had helped him remodel not so long ago.

"No." Jack met Ellery's eyes and shook his head. "No, I don't."

"What do you think happened?"

"We found her skeleton in one of the so-called secret passages. It's actually a tunnel beneath the house that leads to a cave in the bluffs. The hyoid bone in her neck was fractured, indicating strangulation. It takes time to strangle someone. That doesn't happen by accident."

Ellery nodded, feeling a little sick at the thought of Rebecca's last moments.

"Did he give you any details about what happened that night?"

"Not really. It's possible that twenty years later, he's forgotten a few things. He did say he found out about the party from the flyers and went out to Skull House to see Rebecca. She'd broken off their relationship before she left for college, but I guess it wasn't over for Cyrus, although he was married and had a kid of his own by then. He said he and Rebecca used to meet at Skull House, and that she had discovered the tunnel to the beach. I'm sure it was originally used for smuggling."

"So the legend goes."

"Right. Well, sometimes there's truth in legend. Anyway, that's all Cyrus will say about Rebecca. Our best guess is she wasn't interested in getting back together with Cyrus, and at some point in their disagreement, the Robertson kid walked in on them. It's possible he caught Cyrus in the act of strangling Rebecca. It had to be something pretty drastic because Cyrus admits to hitting him over the head with a bronze umbrella stand."

"An umbrella stand?"

"One of those big vases they—"

Ellery said, "No, I know what an umbrella stand is. I thought Steve was killed with a bust of John Mansfield?"

"No. That was a story that Cyrus apparently helped spread over the years. It turns out the umbrella stand has been in the police evidence locker the whole time."

"You're kidding."

Jack's expression was wry. "I wish."

"What's going to happen to Cyrus now?"

"Philippa has filed for divorce, that's one thing that's happened to him. He refused to step down as mayor—"

"He refused?"

"Yep. The town council removed him and has temporarily made Nan mayor."

"Nan is our assistant mayor? How did I not know that?"

"I don't know. She's been assistant mayor for the past eight years. I don't think she has any interest in being mayor, though. She's demanding they hold an election ASAP."

Ellery smiled faintly. He said, "I guess that wraps everything up. Thanks for coming by to fill me in."

"Uh, sure," Jack said. He looked at his empty coffee cup, glanced at the still full coffeepot, and then sighed. "I should really be getting back."

"Of course," Ellery said. He rose from the table at once. Jack rose also.

Watson also stood up, looking hopefully from one to the other.

Jack seemed to hesitate, but then he turned and headed for the hall, saying, "The place is really coming along. Congratulations."

"Thanks," Ellery said. "I'm happy with it."

Not happy about everything, but yes, he was happy with the house. Happy that life seemed to have largely returned to normal, certainly happy that he wasn't lying dead in a secret tunnel beneath Skull House.

"I'm thinking of donating Skull House to the Historical Society," Ellery said as they reached the front door.

"*Donating* it?"

"I don't know what else to do with it. I can't imagine anyone would want to buy it. Especially now."

Jack answered vaguely, "Yeah, well, I'm not an expert in real estate."

Ellery opened the door. He glanced at Jack. Jack was watching him with an oddly intent expression that warmed his face and made his heart beat faster.

"Was there something else?" Ellery asked. He couldn't help hoping there was, even though he was very tired of Jack's on-again-off-again behavior.

"No," Jack said.

To his own astonishment, Ellery heard himself blurt, "Jack, can I ask you something?"

Jack looked a little wary, but he said, "Of course."

"What happened between us?" He hadn't meant to put it quite so bluntly. So honestly. Ellery felt instantly hot, as though he'd jumped into boiling water. He said hastily, "I mean, there was no *us*. I get that. I just mean, what happened the night we went out? Because I thought…"

What a bad idea to start this. What did he think he was going to hear? How would it hurt less to have Jack put into words what Ellery already knew?

"Never mind," Ellery said quickly. "I don't know why I asked. I know the answer."

"No, I'm glad you brought it up," Jack said.

He didn't look glad. He looked grave and pained, and Ellery's heart squeezed so tight, he thought he was going to end then and there. Nobody who looked like that was going to tell you anything you wanted to hear.

"I had a really nice time that night," Jack said. "In fact, it's been years since I had such a nice evening."

Nice. The word of doom. Ellery was nodding like one of those bobblehead dolls on steroids. *Yup, yup, yup. No need to say more.*

Jack sighed, and it was such a weary sound, like the autumn breeze whispering down the chimney, stirring the ashes.

"I was looking at your face in the candlelight. The shine in your eyes and the way you smile. I was listening to your voice, and your laugh, and I could picture you sitting across from me in five years, in ten years, in twenty years... I could see it so clearly." Jack hadn't been looking at Ellery, but he looked at him then, looked into his eyes. "And...I knew I wasn't ready, couldn't face it...caring that much again." He shook his head in regret, in apology.

This was so not remotely what Ellery had expected, he couldn't come up with anything to say.

"I'm sorry. I should have just told you what was going on."

"But then Brandon was murdered, and I was a suspect again," Ellery said. Finally, Jack's inexplicable withdrawal made sense. It was still painful—he really had liked Jack—but as rejection went, it was probably one of the gentler ones.

"Yes. And the last thing either of us needed was a further complication."

Neither of them spoke for a moment.

At last, Ellery nodded. "Thanks for being honest. I did wonder what I'd done wrong."

"Nothing. You did nothing wrong," Jack said. His smile was crooked. "Maybe that's the problem."

Yeah. Well... Ellery was going to leave that right where it lay. Jack had been perfectly clear about what he wanted and needed. It would be a mistake to let attraction and liking cloud the situation.

Ellery had never been a great actor, but he gave his finest performance then. He smiled, tilted his head quizzically. "So. Now that we're on the same, er, page. Any reason we can't still be friends?"

Jack's eyes widened in surprise, and then he smiled. "No. No reason at all. I just assumed—"

"There was no getting over you?" Ellery teased.

Jack reddened, laughed sheepishly again in acknowledgment. "Something like that."

Ellery slapped his hand against his heart. "It won't be easy. It may cost you a week's worth of caramel lattes."

Jack laughed. He looked hopeful and a little confused. "It's a small price to pay for your friendship."

"Okay, then. Well. See you tomorrow?"

Jack studied him for a long moment. Then, to Ellery's astonishment, Jack put a hand on his shoulder, drew him in, and lightly brushed his mouth with his own. Just for an instant, Ellery felt the warm press of mouth on mouth, the softness of lips, the hard bump of cheek and chin, the flick of eyelashes, and then Jack let him go and stepped back.

"See you tomorrow," Jack agreed.

Ellery waited in the doorway, the sea breeze cool against his flushed cheeks, still smiling—his mouth still tingling—till Jack's taillights disappeared into the twilight.

He sighed and glanced down at Watson. Watson smiled up at him, tongue lolling, and wagged his tail.

MYSTERY AT THE MAQUERADE

SECRETS AND SCRABBLE BOOK THREE

Ellery Page, aspiring screenwriter, reigning Scrabble champion, and occasionally clueless owner of the Crow's Nest mystery bookshop, is both flattered and bemused when he's invited to the annual Marauder's Masquerade, the biggest social event of the season in the quaint seaside village of Pirate's Cove, Rhode Island.

Ellery doesn't even know Mrs. Bloodworth-Ainsley—nor, it turns out does Mrs. Bloodworth-Ainsley know Ellery. But Marguerite's son, Julian, *wants* to know him. Julian, handsome, rich, and engaging, is a huge mystery buff, but he's never quite worked up the nerve to ask Ellery out.

As his relationship with Police Chief Jack Carson seems to be dead in the water, Ellery is grateful for a little flattering male attention from the village's most eligible bachelor. But any hopes of romance hit the shoals when Julian is accused of murdering his mother's unlikable second husband during the spooky annual ghost hunt in the old cemetery.

AUTHOR'S NOTE

Dear Reader,

Welcome back to Pirate's Cove, where sinister secrets are buried deeper than Mrs. McGillicuddy's tulips. But also, we never run out of cupcakes! *Secret at Skull House* is the second book in the new M/M cozy mystery series Secrets and Scrabble. As with all cozy mysteries, there is no on-screen violence or sex. That's a rule, not a guideline. To that point—and anticipating your feelings—there are also no sweary words. There are no politics in this world. There is no COVID19. According to the rules of the game (by *game*, I mean the cozy genre, not Scrabble), the stories are quick, light, and fun. This may not be your cup of tea, but in these trying times, I find myself turning more and more often to the reassuring comfort of frequent murder in a world where justice always prevails, good will triumphs, and love will *usually* find a way. So come shelter in place with me for an hour or two; let today's storm pass us by.

The stories are set on fictional Buck Island. The character of Watson is based on my own newly adopted pup Spenser (formerly known as Watson).

Thank you a million-billion times over to Keren. Thank you to Kevin for keeping the home fires burning. Thank YOU, dear readers. Please, please take care of yourselves.

ABOUT THE AUTHOR

Author of over sixty titles of classic Male/Male fiction featuring twisty mystery, kickass adventure, and unapologetic man-on-man romance, JOSH LANYON'S work has been translated into twelve languages. Her FBI thriller *Fair Game* was the first Male/Male title to be published by Harlequin Mondadori, then the largest romance publisher in Italy. *Stranger on the Shore* (Harper Collins Italia) was the first M/M title to be published in print. In 2016 *Fatal Shadows* placed #5 in Japan's annual Boy Love novel list (the first and only title by a foreign author to place on the list). The Adrien English series was awarded the All Time Favorite Couple by the Goodreads M/M Romance Group. In 2019, *Fatal Shadows* became the first LGBTQ mobile game created by Moments: Choose Your Story.

She is an Eppie Award winner, a four-time Lambda Literary Award finalist (twice for Gay Mystery), An Edgar nominee, and the first ever recipient of the Goodreads All Time Favorite M/M Author award.

Josh is married and lives in Southern California.

Find other Josh Lanyon titles at www.joshlanyon.com, and follow Josh on Twitter, Facebook, Goodreads, Instagram and Tumblr.

For extras and exclusives, join Josh on Patreon.

ALSO BY JOSH LANYON

NOVELS

The ADRIEN ENGLISH Mysteries
Fatal Shadows • A Dangerous Thing • The Hell You Say
Death of a Pirate King • The Dark Tide
So This is Christmas • Stranger Things Have Happened

The HOLMES & MORIARITY Mysteries
Somebody Killed His Editor • All She Wrote
The Boy with the Painful Tattoo • In Other Words...Murder

The ALL'S FAIR Series
Fair Game • Fair Play • Fair Chance

The ART OF MURDER Series
The Mermaid Murders •The Monet Murders
The Magician Murders • The Monuments Men Murders

The SECRETS AND SCRABBLE Series
Murder at Pirate's Cove • Secret at Skull House

OTHER NOVELS
The Ghost Wore Yellow Socks
Mexican Heat (with Laura Baumbach) • Strange Fortune
Come Unto These Yellow Sands • This Rough Magic
Stranger on the Shore • Winter Kill • Murder in Pastel
Jefferson Blythe, Esquire • The Curse of the Blue Scarab
Murder Takes the High Road • Séance on a Summer's Night
The Ghost Had an Early Check-Out

NOVELLAS
The DANGEROUS GROUND Series
Dangerous Ground • Old Poison • Blood Heat
Dead Run • Kick Start • Blind Side

The I SPY Series
I Spy Something Bloody • I Spy Something Wicked
I Spy Something Christmas

The IN A DARK WOOD Series
In a Dark Wood • The Parting Glass

The DARK HORSE Series
The Dark Horse • The White Knight

The DOYLE & SPAIN Series
Snowball in Hell

The HAUNTED HEART Series
Haunted Heart Winter

The XOXO FILES Series
Mummie Dearest

OTHER NOVELLAS
Cards on the Table • The Dark Farewell •The Darkling Thrush
The Dickens with Love • Don't Look Back • A Ghost of a Chance
Lovers and Other Strangers • Out of the Blue
A Vintage Affair • Lone Star (in Men Under the Mistletoe)
Green Glass Beads (in Irregulars) • Blood Red Butterfly
Everything I Know • Baby, It's Cold • A Case of Christmas
Murder Between the Pages • Slay Ride

SHORT STORIES

A Limited Engagement • The French Have a Word for It
In Sunshine or In Shadow • Until We Meet Once More
Icecapade (in His for the Holidays) • Perfect Day
Heart Trouble • In Plain Sight • Wedding Favors
Wizard's Moon • Fade to Black • Night Watch
Plenty of Fish • The Boy Next Door
Halloween is Murder

COLLECTIONS

Stories (Vol. 1) • Sweet Spot (the Petit Morts)
Merry Christmas, Darling (Holiday Codas)
Christmas Waltz (Holiday Codas 2)
I Spy...Three Novellas
Point Blank (Five Dangerous Ground Novellas)
Dark Horse, White Knight (Two Novellas)
The Adrien English Mysteries
The Adrien English Mysteries 2

www.ingramcontent.com/pod-product-compliance
Lightning Source LLC
Chambersburg PA
CBHW071241190726
48292CB00007B/2375